GRANNY SKEWERS A SCOUNDREL

(A Fuchsia, Minnesota Mystery)

by

Julie Seedorf

To My Forever Best Friend. May you always keep the sparkle of life and love of your heart.

Love Julie

For information, email **Cozy Cat Press**, cozycatpress@aol.com or visit our website at: www.cozycatpress.com

COZY CAT
P R E S S

ISBN: 978-1-939816-38-2
Printed in the United States of America

Cover design Keri Knutson
http://www.alchemybookcover.blogspot.com
1 2 3 4 5 6 7 8 9 10

I would like to thank Boneyard Coffee & Tea and Latte Da in Champaign, Illinois, for the use of their name in Granny's adventures.

I would also like to thank Amy Beth Arkawy for the use of her book *Dead Silent* for Granny's reading pleasure.

I would also like to thank Cozy Cat Press and Patricia Rockwell for helping me reach my dream.

I dedicate this book to my friend Jan who with her courage in the way she lives her life, gives me courage to journey into the future.

CHAPTER ONE

When Granny ran out of her house into the middle of the street, all she could do was stare. She forgot she was wearing her purple and red velvet-trimmed nightie that was decorated with pink bows. She forgot that she had left her home without her umbrella to protect her. She forgot that Mavis' shade was pulled down and George's boxer shorts were hanging on the pole outside of Mavis' house. All Granny could do was stand frozen in the middle of the street looking at Sally's house.

In all the years Granny had known Sally, she had never seen Sally's yard looking like this. Granny shook her head to clear out the cobwebs, wondering if she was hallucinating, or if she was suffering lasting effects from the perfumed smell that had knocked her out in the tunnels underneath Fuchsia yesterday, and put her in the clutches of the kidnappers and thieves.

Granny tried to remember if she had made her usual bed check of her neighbors' houses the night before as she usually did. It was Granny's job to keep the neighborhood safe. Every morning and every evening Granny checked on her neighbors.

Granny would haul out her binoculars and make sure that Mavis, who lived right across the street, was up and kicking in the morning and ready to get some shut eye in the evening. Mavis usually put on an exhibition or a show for Granny so Granny would know she was ok. Mavis had always wanted to be in a reality television show so she decided to create her own reality TV show for Granny's eyes.

George, who lived next door to Mavis and catty corner on one end of the street from Granny, hung a pair of boxer shorts on a pole outside his door each morning so Granny would know George was ready for the day. Although lately, George's boxer shorts had been looking a little unusual and had gotten very colorful as of late. Sally, the neighbor on the other side of Mavis and across the street catty corner from Granny, the opposite end from George, always put her shade up in the morning and down in the evening so Granny would know that Sally was up and as Sally would always state, "The grass was still talking to her."

In all her excitement, Granny could not remember if she had checked on her neighbors last night. That wasn't unusual for Granny to be forgetful. Some of the time Granny forgot that she forgot. Granny's memory occasionally had a little fog in it. She would forget her car, she would forget her cane, or her umbrella which she occasionally used for a cane, and sometimes she would forget the correct spelling of the name of the town she lived in—Fuchsia, Minnesota. On occasion Granny would spell it Fuschcia. When people called her on getting the name wrong she would tell them that she was reinventing the name Fuchsia because there were too many other things that used the spelling such as the color Fuchsia or the flower Fuchsia. Granny even went so far one time to cover up the fact that she couldn't remember the correct spelling of Fuchsia by trying to get the town council to give Fuchsia a double name, stating that the citizens of Fuchsia would then have a choice whether they wanted a pink Fuchsia town or the strange Fuschsia name.

As far as forgetting her cane, she really didn't need it; it was part of her undercover persona. She didn't want everyone to know that she could sprint with the best of them. Who would think that a little old lady like Granny could hook a crook?

All Granny could do was to stare at the weeds that were everywhere in Sally's yard. Weeds were starting to climb over the windows on the basement of the house. There were purple weeds and pink weeds and weeds that wove their way through what had been grass just the other day, but now looked like viney snakes waiting to catch someone in their lair. How had that happened?

Forgetting that she was standing there in her purple and red velvet-trimmed nightie, Granny offered up a silent prayer as she proceeded to Sally's door. Sally would not have let her yard get like this. Sally meticulously took care of her grass. She had recently told Granny, "The grass speaks to me," as Sally was down on her hands and knees with her scissors snipping a little here and there. Granny never could hear the grass talk, so she chalked up Sally's conversation with her grass to Sally having too much time alone since she didn't appear to have any family.

As Granny neared the door, she could see that it was partially open. Why had she left her umbrella at home? Gently Granny eased the door the rest of the way open. Out of the corner of her eye she saw a long knitting needle lying on the floor. Granny quietly bent down and picked up the knitting needle and put it in jab pose. She called out, "Sally, Sally, are you here?" No answer. Granny opened the door wider and quietly stepped into the house. Calling one more time. "Sally, Sally, where are you?" Hearing no answer, Granny got into her swat team mode and proceeded to check the house room by room, poised with knitting needle in hand in case she met a worthy opponent.

After checking all the rooms and finding no sign of Sally or a dastardly despicable villain, Granny put down the knitting needle and looked around. The window shades were up which meant Sally had either already been up for the day or she hadn't put the shades down last night. Granny couldn't remember if she had checked last night.

Granny smelled the dishes in the sink. They couldn't have been there too long because they only smelled a little like leftover tuna. Granny looked down at the floor when she realized she was wearing her purple and red velvet-trimmed nightie decorated with pink bows. Maybe Sally had something in the closet she could borrow while she investigated what happened.

Granny walked back to the bedroom and opened Sally's closet. A sea of green hit her. Most of Sally's clothes were green. Granny supposed they reminded Sally of her grass that talked to her. Muttering to herself, Granny grabbed Sally's green trench coat and threw it on. It was a little big and as Granny was rolling up her sleeves, a loud wail sounded from the back yard. The wail kept building into a loud crescendo.

Granny knew that sound anywhere. Baskerville, an old dog that Granny had inherited last night when his owner was carted off to the hoosegow, must have gotten out when Granny rushed out the door of her house.

Granny picked up the knitting needle she had put down just in case, ran back out the door she had come in and ran to Mavis' back yard, coat flapping as she tried to find Baskerville in the midst of the growing weeds. How could it be so hard to find such a big dog? The weeds were overtaking everything. It was like looking for a needle in a haystack. Granny blindly plowed her way through the weeds, some as tall as corn right before harvest, until she came to the spot where Baskerville was howling. There was Baskerville standing by Sally, who was on the ground covered with weeds.

"Sally, Sally, wake up, wake up!" There was no response. "Baskerville, lick her face." If that didn't wake her up, nothing would.

Baskerville started licking Sally's face, occasionally nuzzling her neck and whining in her ear.

Sally finally started stirring.

"Sally, what happened? How did you get here? Where did these weeds come from.?"

Sally weakly lifted her head, and shakily grabbed Granny's arm. "The grass," she whispered, "It quit talking to me." That was all she could say before she fell back on the ground, silent.

Granny jumped up. "Baskerville, go for help." Baskerville, jowls hanging, sat and looked at her and started howling. "Not now. We need help." Just as the words came out of Granny's mouth, she heard people tromping through the weeds toward her.

"Help, someone help us!" Granny yelled as she looked for her cell phone. Dagnabbit! She had left home so fast that she had forgotten her phone on the table.

At that moment, George and Mavis tromped through the weeds to get to Granny and stopped quickly, almost falling on top of Granny when they found her. Being so short, Granny had also been hidden by the weeds. They were followed by the shysters: Fish, Little White Poodle, Furball and Tank, Granny's menagerie of furry creatures that lived with her.

Fish was Granny's male cat rescued from a Fish Tank, thus the name Fish; Little White Poodle (female, the name says it all); Furball (huge furry female cat); and Tank (male, short, hulky, stubby-legged dog) were brought home by Fish and had recently helped Granny solve the mystery of disappearing store clerks and mysterious shifty people who showed up in Fuchsia.

When the shysters, as Granny always called her group of furry creatures since they were always in trouble, saw Granny and noticed Sally flopped on the ground with closed eyes and not moving in the midst of the weeds, bedlam ensued. Fish started meowing loudly, Little White Poodle started yapping, Furball curled up hissing and clawing and Tank started snorting as if he smelled something bad. George and Mavis started yelling.

Granny pointed the long knitting needle that she held in her hand straight at George's chest. "Stop that hollering or I will stick you up on the end of this needle and leave you to the weeds. Do you have a phone? We need to call for help. I think she's dead."

George and Mavis looked at Granny in shock. Mavis had been about to call 911 when Granny said the dreaded word "dead."

The phone dropped out of Mavis' hand and she burst out with the worst caterwauling Granny had heard since Hildy Buckshaw opened her eyes one morning to find out Granny (Hermiony Vidalia Criony) as she was called in her middle school years, had dyed Hildy's hair red and blue during the night while she was staying over at Hildy's house. Hermiony had always wanted to try red and blue hair but her parents said proper young ladies didn't do that so Hermiony decided to experiment on Hildy to see what it would look like.

Granny caught the phone just as George grabbed Mavis and put her in a huge lip lock to stop her caterwauling. Granny wanted to stare to figure out what was going on between the two of them but she figured she better see if she could save Sally first.

"911, what's your emergency?"

"We need an ambulance at Sally Katilda's house, pronto." In Fuchsia, everyone knew where everyone lived so there was no need for addresses.

"Would that be across from Hermiony Fiddlestat's house?"

"Quit wasting time, Fern. Sally's dying. The weeds got her. We need that ambulance."

"Did you say weeds, Granny?"

"I hear the sirens!"

"Weeds, Granny?"

Granny hung up the cell phone and directed Baskerville "Howl, Baskerville. Howl!!"

Baskerville started wailing the saddest howl Granny had ever heard. He kept howling until the ambulance crew found them among the weeds. They were followed by the Big Guy as Granny called him, also known as Cornelius Ephraim Stricknine, Fuchsia's Lead Detective/Police Chief.

"Good thing Baskerville was howling or we would have never found you," the Big Guy stated.

As the ambulance crew worked on Sally, the Big Guy turned to Granny, George and Mavis.

"I should have known you couldn't stay out of trouble for very long," the Big Guy chided Granny.

"Me? Can I help it if Sally got tangled in some weeds when I wasn't looking? I have been a little busy you know, helping you keep Fuchsia safe." Granny tapped the Big Guy in the chest and gave him her best put out look. "And this is the kind of thanks I get." Granny purposely sniffed and hung her head. "After all, there is Sally, laying there like a lump and you're accusing me of having something to do with it."

Granny turned and watched as one of the paramedics looked up at the Big Guy and shook his head, indicating there was nothing more they could do for Sally. Granny saw the slight gesture the paramedic made and marched over to him and started jabbing him lightly in the chest with the knitting needle she still held in her hand. "You're wrong; keep working! You can't give up; you can't give up!" Granny screamed at the paramedic. "Sally still has too much grass to talk to."

Just as the Big Guy started over to grab Granny, another large man stepped in, seemingly out of nowhere and grabbed Granny away from the startled paramedic who thought he was going to be jabbed to death by an out of control 100-pound old woman.

"Granny, stop, stop." The man shook Granny gently. "Sally is talking to her grass in heaven now."

"Franklin Gatsby, unhand me." Granny stepped away and put the knitting needle between her and Franklin.

Mavis and George huddled in the corner watching Granny unravel, Mavis weeping loudly. George stoically stared, keeping his eyes turned up to the sky, trying to be brave with his emotions for Mavis' sake.

"What are you doing here, Franklin?," asked Granny, still holding him off with the knitting needle.

As Granny's attention was directed at Franklin, the paramedics quietly put Sally's still body on a stretcher and wheeled her through the weeds, occasionally getting tangled in the mangled mess of vegetation that seemed to envelope the stretcher at times, finally reaching the bright-colored Fuchsia Ambulance that would take Sally to the morgue for an autopsy.

"You didn't meet me at Ella's Enchanted Forest at 10:00 a.m. like we had planned. I heard sirens and for some strange—I can't imagine why—feeling, I knew it had to have something to do with you." Franklin raised his eyes to the heavens and shook his head unbelievingly. "And I was right. You were about to skewer a paramedic!" Franklin yelled reaching for Granny as if he wanted to shake her with exasperation.

Granny held up the knitting needle again in defense. "She's dead, Franklin, she's dead. I failed. I failed. I was supposed to be keeping an eye on Sally. Every day I get my binoculars out and I check on them—George, Mavis and Sally. And last night with all the hoopla of hooking the crooks, I must have forgot, and now Sally is dead; she's dead." Granny dropped the knitting needle, dropped to the ground, uncharacteristically sobbing uncontrollably. Baskerville came over beside her and started howling his saddest howl. Fish started licking her face, little white poodle climbed into her lap and started nuzzling her hand, Furball jumped on her head and started purring to comfort her and Tank rolled over on his back, which was a hard thing to do for such a hefty lug of a dog, right next to her side to give her comfort.

The Big Guy turned to George and Mavis to usher them through the weeds back to Mavis' house to question them, turning to Franklin before they left, "I will question Granny after Mavis and George. You can have a few minutes. It appears that Sally died of natural causes trying to take care of her yard. My team will go over everything but I suspect there isn't anything unusual here."

Watching the others leave, Franklin let out a big sigh and sat down in the weeds next to Granny. Franklin Jester Gatsby had moved to Fuchsia, Minnesota, from New York City. He had been a detective and after his wife had died had wanted to move somewhere quieter. He had met Granny a few weeks ago while she was doing her undercover work for the merchants of Fuchsia. She literally kept falling for him. Then Itsy and Bitsy, Franklin's two pets, whom Granny called Furball and Tank, got into the act by teaming up with Fish and little white poodle who were constantly finding clues for Granny to follow about the kidnappings and break-ins in Fuchsia.

It was hard to believe Franklin had only known Granny for a few weeks. She was so much like his mother who drove him crazy. He had no intention of getting drawn in to Granny's investigations but it seemed he couldn't help himself. She drove him crazy too and he had never felt so alive.

"Hermiony," Granny gave Franklin that look; no one called her Hermiony and got away with it, "Hermiony," Franklin repeated, "You can't blame yourself. You probably checked on Sally last night; you just don't remember. You do have that problem occasionally. It was a rough day, you almost got killed, you saved three people and you got yourself a new '57 Corvette Convertible. So you see, you can't remember everything."

"But, Franklin, you would think we would have all noticed all these weeds. Sally's yard is always perfect. How did they grow so fast?"

Franklin helped Granny up off of the ground, taking the knitting needle out of her hand and setting it on the ground, just in case she got her feisty second wind back and decided she was in jabbing mood again, and started to lead her home. The shysters—Franklin also called the menagerie of animals by the shifty name—led the way.

CHAPTER TWO

Fish, the Little White Poodle, Furball and Tank scooted into the house through the pet door that was installed in Granny's front door. Baskerville started to try to scoot in but Granny opened the door before he could get his big lug of a body stuck in the door.

"Franklin, remind me to expand that pet door for Baskerville," said Granny, momentarily forgetting about Sally's death in her concern for Baskerville.

"Granny, if you expand that door to fit Baskerville you might as well take the door off of your house and invite the whole country to 'come on in.'" Franklin chided.

As they stepped into the house, Franklin attempted to help Granny take off the bright green coat that Granny had borrowed from Sally's closet to cover her attire. Granny, realizing the nature of her attire under her the green coat, slapped Franklin's hands and sprinted into her bedroom and slammed the door.

"Dagnabbit, woman, you are just like my mother." Franklin turned and went into the kitchen and started rummaging around, thinking Granny needed something to calm her down.

Granny slumped against her bedroom door and took a breath. "What to do? What to do?"

Granny could hear in her mind Sally's last words to her. "The grass quit talking to me. She had failed Sally. She should have noticed the weeds. She would have known something was wrong and maybe she would have found Sally earlier. Granny wiped the tears from her eyes with the sleeve of Sally's coat.

Giving herself a little time to sniffle and cry seemed to help.

"Hermiony, are you ok in there? Let me in, Hermiony. Let me help you through this."

Hearing Franklin's voice through the door brought Granny straight out of the sniffles, especially hearing him call her Hermiony. No one called her Hermiony anymore. Granny pulled herself away from the door, stood up as straight as someone who is 5' tall could, and answered, "Don't come in or I'll tell the shysters to trip you. Can't a girl have a moment to herself?" Granny asked as she remembered why she had locked herself in her bedroom.

Granny ripped the bright green coat off and hung it in her closet. She discarded her purple and red-trimmed nightie on the floor of her closet and absent mindedly donned her polyester skirt, a clean blouse and her old lady hosiery, pulling the stockings down around her ankles. She was ready to go back to work in her undercover detective job for the Fuchsia merchants. Maybe by catching a few shoplifters her shock at finding Sally would wear off a little and she could figure out what on earth had happened at Sally's house.

Franklin took one look at Granny and stated, "Why are you dressed in your work getup?"

"I'm going to work."

"The Big Guy isn't going to expect you to patrol the town today after your experience catching the kidnappers yesterday, plus finding Sally today. And no one else will miss you if you're not there. No one in Fuchsia, except now me and the merchants know what you do. No one else in Fuchsia is going to miss an old lady shopping."

Granny gave no inkling that she had heard him and walked over to pick up her umbrella that she used for a cane when she wanted to look feeble. It was also her weapon of choice when she needed to hook a crook.

"You walking or driving?" Franklin asked Granny with a twinkle in his eye and then he winked at Granny.

"Are we back to that winking nonsense, Franklin Gatsby? You should know by now it doesn't work. Now get out of my way. And for your information, I'm walking."

"You might want to change into your sparkly high tops. We're supposed to get rain later today and those feathers that you have on your feet might get a little soggy. They might even start honking if they get wet."

Granny looked down at her feet to see that she had on her feet her designer goose feather slippers. The feathers had been dyed red, and little purple rhinestones sparkled in between the feathers. She had the slippers designed specifically to match her red and purple nightie. They were made out of the goose feathers that the geese had dropped at Blue Bird Park. The edges of the slippers were trimmed with pink feathers and on the bottoms of the slippers, which Franklin couldn't see, were embroidered the words, "I'm fluffy, so don't get huffy."

Granny lifted her eyebrows at Franklin, lifted her umbrella as if to strike, turned on a dime, shot into her bedroom, slammed the door and found her red, sparkly high top tennis shoes. She checked herself in her mirror, muttering to herself. "He seems to be more trouble than he's worth, and to think I thought he might be attractive." Granny plopped one of her hats on top of her head and ran right into Franklin as she opened her bedroom door.

As she nudged Franklin out of the way, Baskerville, Fish, the Little White Poodle, Furball, and Tank had been watching Granny and Franklin, and decided to take control of the situation. Baskerville grabbed Granny's hand in his mouth and pulled her to her chair, Little White Poodle nipped at her heels, Fish and Furball both jumped at her lap at the same time, so she fell back sitting in her chair and Tank was ready on the arm to hurl himself into her lap if she tried to get up.

Just at that moment, Franklin handed Granny a glass of warm milk. Granny looked at the milk as if it were something from another planet. Granny never drank milk unless her kids were at her home or they took her out to eat. They wanted to make sure that she got enough calcium and they insisted she drink her milk. Granny always thought it was their way of getting back at her for all those years she spent "raising them up in the way they should go" and making them drink milk to make their bones stronger and not letting them have pop.

"What is this, Franklin? You know I don't drink this stuff. You're not my kids."

"I thought milk might be just the thing to calm you down."

"Calm? Don't I look calm?" Granny took a deep breath, sighed, gave Franklin that meek smile that she always used when she wanted everyone to think she was meek and mild. "Oh, my, Franklin, you are so right; I feel weak. Maybe my kids are right. Maybe I need the wrinkle farm." With that Granny pretended to take a sip of the milk. "Franklin." Granny winked at him. "Would you mind? In all of my sorrow, I left my knitting needle behind at Sally's. Could you see if the police are done with it yet? I don't think I have it in me to go back over there right now." Granny dabbed at her eyes with the hem of her blouse. "I'll quietly drink my milk and maybe I will take a day off." Granny lowered her eyes and made a small sobbing sound.

"Finally, you're being sensible. I didn't know you were in to knitting. While I'm there, I think I'll look around too. I miss my detective days in New York. Never know when the Big Guy could use another eye."

Franklin looked at the shysters and Baskerville. "Keep her here, Itsy and Bitsy. Baskerville, guard the door and don't let her out. Little White Poodle, sit on her feet, Fish, on her head. Got that?"

The five furry creatures started wagging their tails in understanding. Franklin took one look back at them and walked out the door to Sally's house.

CHAPTER THREE

Granny watched Franklin walk out the door. "Itsy, Bitsy!" Granny looked at Tank who was sitting at her left arm and petted Furball who was sitting next to Fish on her lap. "He still hasn't learned that you have new names fitting your hero status." Furball and Tank were actually Franklin's furry pets but Fish had brought them home one day, and now they spent their days, all four of them, alternating between Granny's house and Franklin's abode. Granny wondered what choices Baskerville would make since he became a part of this menagerie yesterday when his owner was carted off to the hoosegow.

Granny stopped petting Furball and reached underneath her sofa cushion with her hand. She pulled out a large bone and a pack of tuna treats. This got the shysters' attention. First she threw the bone into the kitchen. Tank, Baskerville and Little White Poodle took off, all three reaching the bone at almost the same time. Little White Poodle grabbed the large bone and started dragging it across the floor, Tank and Baskerville trounced behind Little White Poodle trying to catch up and steal the bone.

Granny saw her chance and dumped the entire bag of tuna treats on the floor. Furball and Fish meowed their ninja attack meow and pounced on the treats. Granny hopped over the cats, grabbed her umbrella and sprinted out the door, darting off the front porch and in and out of the bushes until she got to her garage. She took one glance across the street before she slipped into the garage. Franklin was heading to Sally's back yard with the Big Guy.

Yep, both '57 red Chevy Corvettes were there. She hadn't imagined that she had acquired a second Red Chevy Corvette yesterday. She hadn't imagined she had parked in her garage last night. Occasionally, Granny forgot where her car was and lately other people had made her think that she was more forgetful than usual by playing tricks on her with her car.

Granny started her car, revving her engine inside the garage with the garage door closed, before putting it in reverse. She wanted to make sure that she made her getaway while Franklin was still in Sally's back yard, or if he was nearby, he didn't know she was making her escape.

"One, two, three," Granny counted as she hit the remote for her garage door on the count of three. The minute the door was raised, just high enough so her car could get out of the garage, Granny put the pedal to the metal, backed up quickly, turning the wheel to the right when she hit the street. Granny slammed on the brakes to stop her backward descent, hit the foot feed and peeled away with a screech that could be heard for blocks.

Not bad for an old lady, Granny thought. She only had a brief moment to look in her rearview mirror and see Franklin and the Big Guy running out from the side of Sally's house before she was out of their sight.

As Granny cruised past Mrs. Shrill's house on the way to town, out of habit, she slowed the car to see what she could do to aggravate Mrs. Shrill and get a "tut, tut, tut" out of her. Then Granny remembered that Mrs. Shrill was no longer there. She wondered what would happen to the house.

Granny parked in front of AbStract, the department store in Fuchsia that sold anything and everything, plus items unique to Minnesota. Usually it was her first stop on her undercover detective meanderings, but this morning Granny only peered in the window. She stopped and turned around to check to make sure the top was up on the car because it looked like rain. Granny never could remember once she left the car if the top was up or down without looking unless her hair was covering her eyes from the wind whipping her hair while cruising with the top down. Once she was sure all was well with her red '57 Chevy convertible, she meandered down the street and into Ella's Enchanted Forest to have a cup of coffee and a twirled, lemon meringue donut.

Ella's Enchanted Forest had the most delicious coffee drinks and sweet goods in this part of Minnesota and probably the entire nation except for Latte Da in Illinois. Granny had heard that this coffee house in Champaign was the best. Latte Da featured coffee made with beans roasted at their other business called Boneyard Coffee & Tea, but Granny hadn't had the time to take a trip and visit since catching the crooks in Fuchsia took all of her time. Ella's also had plants and a forest growing out of part of her building; at least she did until recently when the forest had disappeared. Ella's had always been an oasis with the ambiance of a garden atmosphere. Granny wondered, as she walked in the door and saw the empty Forest Room, what Delight Delure and her daughter Ella, who the establishment was named after, would do with the room now. Maybe she would ask Granny for her forest back.

As Granny walked in the door, Delight threw her hands into the air and ran up to Granny, started hugging her, lifting Granny off of her feet. Delight was a little hefty and Granny being a tiny slip of a thing was easy to lift off of the ground and be twirled around. Granny held on to her hat with one hand and used the umbrella she was holding in the other hand to reach out and hook the edge of the counter so Delight would stop the twirling.

Delight set Granny down and while Granny held on to the counter for dear life to stop the spinning, Delight started giving orders to her daughter Ella. "Granny gets free coffee and lattes for the rest of her life. Bring her a latte and the specialty donut I made for her full of whipped cream, caramel, chocolate drops, and put five scoops of five different ice creams on top." Delight held out a chair. "Sit here, Granny, and we will take good care of you." Delight invited Granny as she dusted off the chair.

Granny, having never been accustomed to being greeted this way when entering Ella's, kept Delight in line's eye as she slowly lowered herself down on the chair. "You feelin' ok, Delight?"

At those words, Delight swept down and again grabbed Granny in a bear hug, rocking back and forth and back and forth as she hugged Granny.

Granny, feeling like a banana being squished out of its peel, managed to slide her umbrella up far enough to touch Delight's arms and unhook Delight's left arm from her body. Granny then was loose enough to slide down to the ground off of the chair and out of Delight's arms.

"Oh, my goodness. Granny, what happened?"

Granny lay down on the floor on one arm, looking up at the underside of the table, trying to come up with an explanation so as to not hurt Delight's feelings. "I was thinking that you should paint the underside of your tables fuchsia and carry the color up the edges to accent the white on the top of the table. It would brand your coffee nook as the Fuchsia of Minnesota coffee houses."

Delight lay down on the floor next to Granny and looked at the underside of the table. "You're right, Granny. What a great idea!"

Delight did not see Granny roll her eyes as she used her umbrella to hoist herself back up and sit down in the chair. "Delight, what's with the hugging?"

"You saved my daughter's life, Granny. She could have died, all because she fell for some good looking, fast talking, present bearing lothario." Delight started sobbing.

"She's safe now and did you see that cute policeman I had escort her home from the crime scene?" Granny replied, trying to distract Delight onto another subject as Ella set the latte and desert on the table in front of Granny.

Granny was about to take her first bite when the Mayor of Fuchsia, Horatio Helecort, and the entire Fuchsia City Council strolled in the door and headed for the former Forest Room in Ella's.

"What's that all about?" Granny asked Delight.

"They told me they were coming. They have to make some big decisions about what they should do with the new streets that you discovered underneath Fuchsia. Should they be boarded up? Should they be used? I bet this is something in their wildest dreams that they never ever thought they would have to deal with."

Granny could tell Delight something about wildest dreams but a girl still needed to have some secrets.

"Here you are, Granny." The Big Guy bustled in the front door. "What was with the screeching tires? Did you want a ticket?"

Granny sighed and took a swig of the latte, wishing something stronger had been put in the latte. It was only 9:00 a.m. and it felt like the midnight of doomsday.

"I had to work, Cornelius. I kept seeing Sally tangled in the weeds so I had to work and I knew you and Franklin would try to stop me."

"Or you knew I would want to question you and you were trying to avoid me because you know more than you're letting on."

"What could I know? Sally's dead, the grass quit talking to her and I failed to help her in her time of need."

"Granny, tell me why you went over to Sally's house."

"I took my binoculars and looked out my window and Sally's lawn was covered in weeds. Sally does not let weeds grow. I ran over to her house and her door was unlocked. I called her name and she didn't answer so I went in. There was no one there."

Granny decided to leave out the part of sneaking into Sally's closet and borrowing Sally's green coat. The coat didn't have anything to do with it anyway and why expose her eclectic bedroom attire to the one who hauled the crooks away after she caught them. She didn't want him to be distracted by thinking about her in lingerie from Red Hot Momma's Boutique.

"Then I heard this awful caterwauling. Baskerville must have followed me out of my house and he was in the back yard making this gad awful noise. I ran back to where he was and there was Sally, all tangled in weeds." Granny started coughing to hide the fact that she might be ready to break down crying and Granny never cried unless she wanted to fool someone.

"What happened next, Granny?" the Big Guy inquired handing her a glass of water.

Granny took a gulp, wishing again it were something stronger. "I knelt down beside Sally. She woke up, grabbed my arm, lifted her head and said to me, "The grass quit talking to me." Her head fell back and she was gone. Granny hung her head in silence.

"When did George and Mavis arrive?"

"They heard Baskerville and came running. We called 911 and you know the rest."

"Explain to me why Sally told you the grass quit talking to her."

"She always went on about her grass and told me it talked to her. She was a little daffy at times, happens to all of us," Granny said with a helpless look.

"Do you want me to drive you home and you can get your car later? This has been a lot for a woman of your age to take in. I think you should go home and rest."

At the word *rest,* Granny's head popped up and she stuck her jaw out, got a stubborn look on her face and stood up. She stomped her umbrella on the ground right next to the Big Guy's foot, made a huffing sound and while walking out the door said, "I'm not Sally, I'm not dead and you see my shoes? They're red. Enough said!" Granny loved rhyming. She didn't know what all that meant but neither did the Big Guy and it was enough to scare him to leave her alone.

The Big Guy stood up and walked out behind Granny. He watched her walk down the street, knowing when Granny was in that mood, trouble was bound to follow.

CHAPTER FOUR

Granny headed down the main street of Fuchsia with no destination in mind. She was in such deep thought that she didn't see Ditty Belle sweeping the sidewalk in front of the bookstore that Ditty owned—Persnickety's. Granny had been using her umbrella to guide her steps when she felt the umbrella become entangled in something. Thinking she was being accosted by a pickpocket, Granny raised her umbrella ready to strike at the same time Ditty Belle thought she was being mugged and raised her broom to strike.

Umbrella and broom in the air, both women looked up just in time to save both of themselves a good conk on the head.

"Ditty!"

"Granny!"

They both exclaimed at the same time, weapons paused in the air.

"Ditty, what do you think you are doing trying to strike an old woman?"

"Granny, I'm so sorry," Ditty exclaimed, lowering her broom. "What with all the goings on in Fuchsia the last couple of days, I'm a little skittish."

Granny lowered her umbrella. "Well, I hooked those crooks, and you're safe now. Just got lucky being a little old lady and all. Who would have thought I would remember long enough to solve the crime?"

"Granny, I'm one of the merchants remember? Or perhaps you don't. You work for us. We know your secret. But we've all been instructed not to let the cat out of the bag that you are our undercover person for spotting shoplifters and crooks. The police and the Big guy are telling everyone that you were in the right place at the right time and got lucky."

"That's good. I was worried I'd be out of a job. How'd you hear that? I just saw the Big Guy and he didn't say anything."

"Well, Granny, did you forget? Sally was murdered. I'm sure he's got other things on his mind. But don't you remember? You were there?"

"There? Where? Sally wasn't murdered, she died, had a heart attack or something. Quit spreading rumors Ditty!"

Granny turned and stomped back in the direction she had come from. *Murdered? Sally wasn't murdered. Or was she? What weren't they telling her?*

Granny picked up the pace, practically sprinting past Ella's Enchanted Forest, until she remembered she was supposed to be old so she slowed her step and kept on walking. She walked right past AbStract and on down the street toward home. Home was about a mile away so it wasn't far on the days Granny decided to walk to town.

She was careful not to step on the cracks in the sidewalk. She couldn't get the nursery ditty out of her mind. Step on the cracks, you break your mother's back. Something like that was hard to forget, so no matter how old she was, she always avoided the cracks. Granny also noticed that leaves were starting to fall from the trees. Summer was over. She had been so busy, caught up in the goings on of the crooks and the underground streets that she had failed to notice the time passing and fall arriving.

As Granny got closer to her house, she saw something strange wiggling by her front door. Slowly and cautiously, she climbed the front steps to her house.

A loud howl made her jump. Baskerville had tried to get into the house through the pet door and was stuck.

"I knew I needed to make that door bigger for you, Baskerville," Granny said to the hound as she leaned down to see what she could do to get him unstuck. Granny slid her slim arms around his backside and gave a tug. Even though she was tiny, Granny had muscles. She lifted weights so she would be a match if the bad guys ever got physical.

"Baskerville, I think we need some help from the garage; be patient." Granny turned back down the steps and headed for her garage. Baskerville gave a low moan as if to say, "I trust you, Granny." Granny thought that it was nice to have at least one creature trusting her. It was a good thing the other shysters didn't seem to be around or the racket would have woke the dead and since the cemetery was right behind her house, well, who knew what ghosts lingered there?

As Granny opened the door to the garage, she had a vague feeling that she had forgot something, but she couldn't quite put her finger on it. Once inside the garage, she looked around for something greasy to grease down Baskerville. As she scoped out her garage, she realized what she had forgotten. There was only one red '57 Chevy in the garage. She had forgotten that she had driven downtown this morning and now her car was stranded on Main Street.

"Well, I'll just drive my other car downtown to get it when I get Baskerville unstuck," she thought absentmindedly. Granny walked over to her workbench and started tossing the items on top of it to and fro. Finally at the bottom of the pile she came upon just the thing—Vaseline. Cooking oil would have been much better, but because Baskerville was stuck in the door, she couldn't get in the front door. Before she had left home she had moved her cedar chest, that she kept by the back door for boots and mittens, in front of the door so she could climb on it and reach the hidden key for the secret door in the basement, in case she needed to come home that way. Getting in the back door was out of the question because she had forgotten to put the chest back in its rightful place and it still blocked the door. If she used the hidden basement door she would have to go back downtown, wind through the underground streets and get in that way. She wasn't sure Baskerville could last that long.

For a second, she picked up the WD-40 but put it back down. Toxic chemicals would not be good for Baskerville. Granny picked up the Vaseline, hurried back to her porch, talked soothingly to Baskerville while she rubbed him down with Vaseline. Then she gave a good count. "One, Two, Three." One shove and Baskerville was through the door, Vaseline and all.

Granny turned to see if she had left a towel on the porch when she was watering her plants to clean her hands so she could get the doorknob open. She would have to teach Baskerville how to open the door. As Granny turned, she noticed her potted Fuchsia plant. It had a knitting needle stuck deep in the soil skewered to a note attached. It sounded ominous:

"Don't needle me any more, Granny. I won't be responsible for my actions." It was signed Franklin.

Granny picked up the knitting needle and eyed it suspiciously before she proceeded into her house. She had had enough hoopla for the day but she still had to rescue her car from Main Street before anyone realized that she had forgotten it and she had to clean off the Vaseline from Baskerville before he greased everything in her house and before he licked it off of himself and got sick.

Granny sat down and flipped open her laptop computer and headed straight to etellme.com. *Ooh, this is going to get messy*, Granny thought. First she was supposed to cover his fur with a large layer of liquid dish detergent, then dampen a soft cloth with water, then wipe off the dish detergent with the soft, wet cloth and keep repeating the steps until the greasiness was gone.

Granny thought maybe she had picked the wrong item to use to squeeze Baskerville through the door. How in the world was she going to get him to sit long enough to do that? She needed to think, but fast.

Granny dug in her refrigerator and brought out the big steak that her kids had left her last time they had visited. She led Baskerville to her Jacuzzi tub in the bathroom because it also had one of those doohickey nozzles that moved. She coaxed Baskerville into the tub with the steak and put the steak by the farthest wall of the tub. As Baskerville was nibbling on the steak Granny doused him with dish detergent and started rubbing his fur with the soft wet cloth. She had started to rinse him off with the doohickey when a loud pounding on the door began. Baskerville jumped at the same time as Granny jumped, making them collide in midair. Granny toppled in the tub on top of Baskerville and the doohickey nozzle Granny had been holding slipped out of Granny's hands, became uncontrollable, and started spraying them and the bathroom. It was a snake striking anyone that got in its way.

Just at that moment, the door opened. Granny looked up to see three mouths wide open in shock and three sets of eyes that mimicked owl eyes trying to see at night. Her kids were here.

CHAPTER FIVE

Penelope, Granny's older daughter, ran to the tub and grabbed Granny. Thor, Granny's son, ran and grabbed Baskerville. Starshine, Granny's middle child, grabbed a towel and hopped up and down on her two feet, not sure what to do with the towel.

"Grab him, Thor," Penelope shouted, "before he attacks mom anymore." At the same time, she jumped in the tub and put herself between Granny and the big dog.

Baskerville, startled by this rude interruption started howling a howl that would bring a city to its knees if he were outside. Thor tried to get a firm grip on Baskerville's collar but his hands kept slipping off. Thor then tried to get his arms around Baskerville's big neck but his grasp kept slipping off of Baskerville's greasy neck. Baskerville, having had enough of this and being scared for his life, jumped out of the tub and ran out the door grabbing the towel that Starshine held in her hands, knocking Starshine down in the process.

"What are you doing?" Granny yelled in a loud voice. "Unhand me, Penelope!" Granny lifted up her arms and lifted her feet, sparkly tennis shoes and all and hauled herself out of the tub, stepping over the shocked Starshine, and tromped down the hall trying to catch Baskerville.

It took Penelope and Thor a moment to shake and dry themselves off and follow Granny down the hall, a trail of water puddling on the floor from their soggy clothes, so that when Starshine started to follow, hopping from anxiety, her hopping feet made splashes on the wall.

Granny was first to the front door where Baskerville was again stuck in the doggy door trying to escape the madness in the house. "Now look what you've done!" Granny proclaimed to her children. As Granny turned to confront them she caught a glimpse of Fish, Little White Poodle, Tank and Furball hiding behind the couch waiting to make their getaway to hide under Granny's bed until her children were gone. The shysters knew her children didn't know about them so they always hid when her family decided to visit.

"Now look what you've done. He's stuck again."

"What is that monster and why is he here?" Penelope asked.

"You know all that hoopla last night that was reported in the news? The one where we caught some crooks and I accidently got involved? Well, his owner was arrested and the crooks' dog likes me and I like him. And all of you always worry about me being safe so I thought he would be good protection." Granny explained innocently.

At that moment, Baskerville, tired of being stuck in the door gave out a huge howl.

Thor, grabbed the towel that Baskerville had grabbed from Starshine, which was now hanging from Baskerville's tail and used it to keep himself from sliding off of Baskerville's Vaseline greased body so he could pull Baskerville out of the door. Baskerville immediately ran over to Starshine and jumped up hugging her shoulders and licking her face.

"He loves me. Oh," Starshine said with a smitten grin on her face.

"What are all of you doing here, scaring me to death?"

Penelope, Thor and Starshine all gave a sigh at the same time. "Sit down, Mom," Starshine instructed her mother. "We've come to talk to you about something. And it seems this conversation is taking place none too soon."

Penelope sat Granny down in her chair and took her hand. "You know we worry about you, Mom. You could have been killed last night. You know we have been concerned you shouldn't be living alone."

Thor knelt down beside Granny, Starshine followed his lead, kneeling on the other side of Granny and taking her other hand. Baskerville, not wanting to be left out, put his paws on the chair cushion behind her head. The shysters hiding behind the couch decided it would be a good time to hide under Granny's bed. They silently crept away to Granny's bedroom unnoticed.

Granny looked at her children suspiciously. With two of them down on their knees and taking her hands, Granny thought it looked as if they were going to propose to her. "What is this all about?"

"We were concerned last night when we heard what happened but we wanted to wait until today to talk to you and then we heard about Sally's murder," Penelope continued on not noticing the change in Granny's face as the word *murder* settled in Granny's brain. "I want you to come and live with me. My kids have left home, Butch is at work all the time and we can take care of you. We've talked it over and it's live with me or the assisted living or the nursing home."

Granny knew she should have been concerned about the word *nursing home* and *assisted living;* she always knew they wanted her in the wrinkle farm but the only thing that registered in Granny's head was the word *murder*.

"Who told you Sally was murdered? I was there, the weeds quit talking to her. Maybe she had a heart attack?"

Propose? They were going to propose all right, propose Granny go to the wrinkle farm. Granny thought as she pulled her hands out of their grasp.

"We'll talk about that later, maybe you should rest. We are going to stay awhile to make sure you are ok and then we will make plans." Starshine gently suggested as she turned and hugged Baskerville.

"And we need to make arrangements for this monster," Penelope decided.

Granny, quickly putting together a plan in her mind, suggested, "Why don't you see what you can find to eat? I am really tired and weak. I am going to rest in the basement in front of the TV. Just give me some time to get my strength back after these nightmare couple of days and we'll talk."

Granny quickly walked to the basement steps. "Don't disturb me for two hours. That should be enough time to recuperate." Granny winked and headed down the steps.

At the bottom of the stairs, Granny paused to listen. The kids were digging into the fridge and commenting on the food Granny had stashed. She knew when they left, she was going to have to go on a shopping trip because they would have replaced the chocolate, ice cream and the donuts with some sort of weird healthy food unless they decided to cart her away first.

Granny quickly and quietly moved to the fireplace. She ran her hand inside the fireplace and found the latch for the secret door that she had found during her previous investigation which led to the streets underneath Fuchsia. There was no time like the present to go downtown and retrieve her car that she had forgotten. The latch opened and she stepped into the secret room, being careful to shut the secret fireplace door behind her. Her kids didn't know about that door yet because they hadn't heard all of the details of yesterday's ruckus. Granny hurried across the room and headed through the door to the underground streets.

CHAPTER SIX

The underground street lamps were still on. The Mayor and City Council of Fuchsia hadn't turned off the lights after the crooks had been caught.

Granny proceeded in the direction of Ella's Enchanted Forest. She found the lift switch for the large elevator lift, got on the floor and rode it up into Ella's.

Delight had been in the process of closing the shop when she heard the lift in the Forest Room being activated. When Granny and the lift became even with the floor, Granny saw a large flower pot being ready to be lowered on her head.

"Delight, it's me," Granny yelled as she held the umbrella that she had thought to grab before she had retreated to her downstairs, up, to ward off the flower pot.

"Goodness gracious, Granny, what are you doing here?"

"It's a long story. Don't have time to explain. Don't tell anyone you saw me." With that Granny proceeded to the front door before Delight had a chance to lower the flower pot from over her head in striking pose.

Granny's car was still parked in the same spot where she had left it in the morning. Granny hopped in her car and slowly drove down the street so as to not draw attention to herself. As she drove, Granny came up with an idea.

Franklin's car was parked in his driveway. Granny grabbed her umbrella and exited the car, taking her time and being a little clumsy getting out. She walked slowly as she shuffled up the sidewalk, giving up a silent prayer because she was shuffling on the cracks, but she had to make it look like she was in need of help in case Franklin was watching from the window.

Granny gave a feeble knock on Franklin's door. There was no answer. She knew he was inside. "Franklin, open up; it's Granny."

"This is Itsy; there's no one home."

"Franklin, you have to open the door; this is important."

The door opened a crack and Franklin stuck his head out the door. "What part of the knitting needle skewered into a note that told you to not needle me anymore didn't you understand?" Franklin asked with an ominous tone as he started to shut the door.

Granny was quick with her umbrella and wedged it in the doorway so the door would not shut.

"It's Itsy and Bitsy; they're in trouble and they need you."

Franklin opened the door a little wider. "I thought they were Furball and Tank?" Franklin asked suspiciously.

"They are, they are, but I'm so rattled and I don't know what to do. They are stuck in my house." Technically Granny thought that was true because they were hiding so Granny's children didn't see them. "And I can't get them out. You should hear the ruckus." Granny didn't tell him the ruckus was from Baskerville being stuck in the door, another small technicality.

The door opened wider. "How did they get stuck? Why did you leave them? Why didn't you call me?"

"They aren't in danger; they just can't get out of a tight spot and my cell phone wasn't charged, and I was so rattled, I didn't think to use my regular phone. You've got to help them, Franklin."

Franklin gave Granny a stern look and tried to judge whether this was another of Granny's antics but he didn't want to take the chance that Itsy and Bitsy really were in trouble.

Granny jumped in her red '57 Chevy Corvette, revved its engine and sped down the street. Franklin, not wanting to let Granny get the best of his black Corvette, kept up with Granny, curbing his instinct to try and pass her and beat her to her house.

When Granny pulled into her garage, her children were on the front porch of her house having an animated discussion. When they saw Granny, they ran down the steps, Baskerville at their heels.

Starshine and Penelope were both chattering so fast and making so many gestures Granny thought their heads were going to spin off of their bodies. Thor on the other hand was standing by, too calm for Granny's liking.

At that moment, Franklin walked up to the anxious group. Granny quickly grabbed his arm and dragged him close to her daughters. She looked at Baskerville and gave a command, "Howl, Baskerville, howl!"

Baskerville let out a blood curdling howl that Granny was sure would wake the dead in the cemetery behind her house. She saw Mavis look out her window pretending to be Marilyn Monroe in one of her reality show fantasies. Was that George in the window too with a Clark Gable wig and mustache?

The silence got Granny's attention away from Mavis' window. "Good job, Baskerville. Now, may I speak?" Granny's serious tone, which was unlike her, commanded Penelope, Starshine, and Thor's attention.

Franklin decided he had better listen too because she didn't seem too concerned about helping Itsy and Bitsy. *Where were they?*

"Penelope, Starshine and Thor, I would like you to meet Franklin." Granny gave a little pause, "My fiancé."

When the word *fiancé* came out of Granny's mouth, Franklin's head popped up and he gave a startled jump. Granny, as little as she was, had strength and she held on to his arm with a death grip so he couldn't move without knocking her down.

"Fiancé!"

"Fiancé!"

"Fiancé!" All three children screamed at the same time.

Franklin and Granny jumped back quickly as the group had advanced on them when they spoke.

"Yes, my fiancé, Franklin Jester Gatsby." We met a few weeks ago. He's a retired New York Police detective who moved to Fuchsia for a quieter life. And he saved my life yesterday. I am in good hands and I would like your blessing. Franklin, don't you have anything to say?" Granny nudged him lightly with her umbrella.

"I..ah...I...yes...ahh...Granny,   ahh   Granny," Franklin choked and coughed out the words.

"He's overcome with emotion from meeting you kids, so you should go. We can arrange another time when you can get to know Franklin better." Granny started leading them toward their car.

Thor walked up to Franklin. "I guess congratulations are in order but we aren't giving our blessing yet."

Penelope stood on her tiptoes and looked Franklin in the eyes. Penelope took after her mother in the shortness category. "You harm one hair on her head and you will answer to us."

Starshine, whose motto was love, walked over to Franklin, stood on her tiptoes, gave him a kiss on the cheek and a big hug. "Hi, Dad."

Before Franklin could unjumble the words running through his head, the three were getting into their car. Thor rolled down the window and gave Granny one more bit of news. "Just so you know, we are going to hold off having you live with Penelope and Butch or taking you to another home. We are going to adopt a wait and see attitude." Thor rolled the window back up and gunned the engine (Granny had taught him to drive) and roared down the street with his sisters screaming in the back at such an abrupt take off.

Granny started pacing and ranting. "All this trouble for nothing. I get to stay in my home. They're leaving me here. They couldn't tell me that before? Good bye, Franklin. I've got things to do."

This time it was Franklin's turn to grab Granny by the arm, only gently. "Do you remember what else I said in my skewered note?"

"Ah, something about not being responsible for your actions?" Granny answered in a weak voice.

"Itsy and Bitsy were never in trouble, were they?" At those words, Fish, Little White Poodle, Furball and Tank came prancing out of the pet door onto the porch. They stopped and looked at Granny and Franklin. Fish gave a meow, Little White Poodle stood on his hind legs and shook his front paws in their direction as if in a wave, Tank gave a low growl and Furball gave a hiss as they ran down the steps and scurried down the street in the opposite direction, leaving Baskerville sitting beside Franklin and Granny. Baskerville, seeing that he was being left behind, reared up and quickly licked Franklin on the cheek, rubbed against Granny on his way down and trounced on down the street after the shysters.

Granny took advantage of the moment and pulled away from Franklin and started up her steps. All of a sudden, she heard roaring laughter. Franklin laughing? Granny turned to see what was so funny. Franklin was laughing so hard he was almost crying.

In between bursts of laughter, Granny could hear the words coming out of Franklin's mouth. "You are the most irascible, infuriating, exciting, crazy woman I have ever met besides my mother. You are driving me crazy and I like it."

Granny's eyes opened wide. This wasn't the reaction she was expecting. She didn't move.

"Come on, Hermiony, as long as we're engaged, I might as well buy you dinner at Rack's to celebrate our engagement. I might even be able to get you an engagement ring out of the penny trinket machine." Franklin bowed, walked over to Granny and held out his hand.

Granny, now suspicious, ignored his hand and walked over to his black Corvette. "I am kind of hungry. Well, what are you waiting for, start the car."

CHAPTER SEVEN

The waitress at Rack's seated Granny and Franklin at Granny's favorite booth towards the back of the restaurant. The booth gave Granny a good view of the other diners. If there was any trouble, Granny could whip out of the booth and stop the shoplifter or crook before they knew what happened. Granny always had some way making it appear as if whatever she did was an accident by a clumsy old woman, but at the same time she would push the remote alarm that she carried, tipping off the Big Guy. He would swoop down and arrest the crook. Granny would feign innocence and go back to what she had been doing. The residents of Fuchsia would shake their heads and accept that it was another Granny moment.

Granny decided to take the night off and not look for trouble. She figured she was already in hot water with Franklin so she had better give him her undivided attention. And…she wanted to find out why everyone kept saying that Sally was murdered.

Granny ordered her usual meal of deep fried onion rings, deep fried chicken and mashed potatoes and gravy from the new waiter. Granny had not seen this waiter before so she gave him a quick wink as she ordered. She needed to train him on her eating habits especially when her daughters were with her. Maizie, the former waitress in Rack's, had known that when Granny's family was with her, the order of the day was healthy food.

"Franklin will have the same," Granny instructed the waiter as she grabbed the menu out of Franklin's hand and gave it back to the waiter.

"How did you know what my favorite foods were, Granny?" Franklin wasn't a big fan of the meal Granny had just ordered for him but he suspected she knew that and was trying to rile him. He winked at Granny and said to the waiter, "And for desert we would like chocolate fudge ice cream with a donut on top."

Granny set her water glass down with a loud thud and glared at Franklin. "What are you up to ordering my favorite dessert? No one orders my favorites for me because they want me to eat healthy. Are you trying to get rid of me by feeding me unhealthy foods so I'll kick the bucket and leave the sleuthing in the town of Fuchsia to you? And that winking isn't going to work."

Franklin's answer to Granny's questions was a big grin.

Granny took a few minutes to give Franklin the silent treatment before her curiosity got the best of her. "Why is everyone saying that Sally was murdered?"

Franklin tapped his fingers on the table before picking up the silverware to still his hands, pausing to take a breath before he broke the news to Granny that he knew would set her on her nosy nosing about.

"The autopsy revealed that she died of strychnine poisoning."

Granny tapped her umbrella on the floor. "Strychnine as in the Big Guy strychnine?" referring to the Big Guy's real name, Cornelius Ephraim Stricknine.

"No, it's spelled differently," Franklin retorted.

Granny glared at Franklin and started lifting her umbrella. "Did the Big Guy kill Sally?"

"I'm talking about the poison. She ingested strychnine. They are still investigating to see how the poison got into her system."

Granny slumped back into the booth. "The grass and weeds didn't kill her. She didn't have a heart attack. But how, and more importantly, why? Why would someone want to poison Sally and how did the weeds appear almost overnight?"

"Not your worry, Granny. Now let's talk about this fiancé thing. Would you mind telling me how I came to be your fiancé?"

Granny glanced out the window next to the booth trying to buy time before she explained about her kids. Granny expected to see Mrs. Periwinkle, who lived across the street from Racks, feeding her squirrels. Granny was a frequent visitor at Rack's at this time of the evening and Mrs. Periwinkle usually fed her squirrels at the same time every evening. The squirrel feeders were full. Granny glanced at the time on her cell phone. It was a little later; Granny had missed the feeding. Granny was about to turn back to answer Franklin when her eyes zeroed in on Mrs. Periwinkle's lawn. What Granny saw made her stand with a jolt.

Granny grabbed her umbrella and before Franklin could open his mouth, Granny took off running out of Rack's as if someone was chasing her. Franklin decided to do just that and knocked over all the water on the table as he exited the booth and took chase after Granny.

Mrs. Periwinkle was about to take a sip from a cup of lavender tea when Granny bounded through her unlocked door. Mrs. Periwinkle's tea had almost made it to her mouth before Granny knocked it out of her hands. Mrs. Periwinkle stood up in surprise, tea dripping down the front of her dress. Granny grabbed Mrs. Periwinkle's shoulders and started pushing her out the door.

"You've got to leave this house, now!" Granny yelled.

Franklin ran in the door that Granny was just about to push Mrs. Periwinkle out of. He caught Mrs. Periwinkle just as she was about to fly through the door from Granny's gentle push.

"Hermiony, what are you doing?"

Mrs. Periwinkle, still being held by Franklin, looked at Granny curiously. "Hermiony?"

"It's Granny to you, Esmeralda Periwinkle," Granny proclaimed with a sharp tone. "She has to leave or she'll die. I am saving her. Come on, Esmeralda." Granny grabbed Mrs. Periwinkle away from Franklin and started to again push her to the door.

"Granny, stop!" Franklin Jester Gatsby then pried Granny's hands off of Mrs. Periwinkle's arms. "Hermiony, we are leaving NOW!" Franklin picked up Granny in a big bear hug and hustled her out of the house, leaving Mrs. Periwinkle standing with her jaw open in astonishment, not quite comprehending what had just happened.

"Put me down! Don't you understand?" Granny screamed as Franklin deposited her in his car. "Look at her grass! There isn't any. There are weeds! Weeds that weren't there a couple of days ago. She's going to die. She's going to die, Franklin, unless I save her."

Franklin made sure the doors were locked solid before he pulled away from the curb. By this time, onlookers had gathered to see what the commotion was. Mrs. Periwinkle stood at the door watching them drive away. Mrs. Periwinkle shook her head in disbelief as she turned back into her kitchen to make a new cup of lavender tea.

As Franklin drove Granny away from Mrs. Periwinkle's house, his mind was on Granny's strange behavior and Granny's children. Franklin hoped this behavior didn't get back to Granny's children or there would be nothing he could do to save her from her kids.

He suspected, even though Granny hadn't told him how he came to be her fiancé, that he was her loophole to avoiding the wrinkle farm.

CHAPTER EIGHT

If there was one thing that could be said about Granny it was the fact that she didn't walk away from a good fight quietly. Franklin had all he could do to keep Granny from hitting him with her umbrella so he would stop the car and she could go back to Mrs. Periwinkle's.

As he pulled up in front of her house, he tried to reason with her. "Hermiony, why in the world would you think Mrs. Periwinkle is going to die?"

"Didn't you see her yard? It looked just like Sally's before she died, fully of creepy, crawly weeds and you told me yourself that Sally was murdered. Strychnine, you said; strychnine. It must have been put in her tea. Esmeralda Periwinkle was drinking tea and if my nose is right, it was the same tea that Sally used to drink, lavender. The weeds were what got my attention, and then when I saw her drinking the tea. I ran over to warn her. I knew. She was next!"

"Hermiony, you have got to calm down. I'll walk you to your house; you need to get a good night's sleep and all will be better in the morning. These last few days have been too hard on you." Franklin tried his most soothing tone and then he winked at Granny. That was his biggest mistake.

Granny quickly opened the car door to Franklin's black '57 Chevy Corvette, and hopped out decisively. "Don't you try that wink on me, Franklin. I am not some doddering old woman who can be fooled by a wink and I am not crazy. If Mrs. Periwinkle dies, it is on your head, do you understand? On your head!"

Granny slammed the car door and gave it a big thunk with her umbrella and stomped up the sidewalk into her house, slamming that door too. The big thunk to his beautiful '57 Chevy made Franklin cringe. *Yup, she was like his mother all right. The difference was that a mother is a mother for life. Granny didn't need to be his wife.*

When Franklin realized he was now starting to think in rhymes like Granny, he stomped on the gas pedal and sped away from Granny's as fast as he could. The thought of starting to think like Granny was enough to drive him to drink and he wasn't a drinking man. *What was happening to him?*

Granny slammed her door and went straight to her fridge and pulled out her bottle of wine. She tossed off her red sparkly high tops and marched into her closet and opened the secret door in the back where she kept her books that she didn't want her children to see and her flip flops when she was out of the house. Granny put her feet in her flip flops and gave a sigh of contentment. She always could think better in her flip flops. Her kids always worried she was going to flip flop on the floor in her flip flops so she had to hide a few pairs around the house as they were always disappearing after her kids visited. Granny figured she liked to live dangerously and what was a flop without a flip?

Before she plopped in her chair to have her wine she realized that it was time to get her binoculars out to check on her neighbors. It was her way of making sure everyone was safe. George across the way and over to the right across the street from Granny always hung boxer shorts on the pole outside of his house in the morning so Granny knew he was alive and kicking. At night he took them down. Mavis straight across the street from Granny didn't like shades so she would

always perform in her own reality TV show in front of
the window. Granny never knew what she would see
when she checked on Mavis.

George was all tucked in. His house was dark and
the boxer shorts were gone. Mavis stood in front of her
window blowing kisses at Granny. Granny wondered
which movie star she was tonight. Then Granny trained
her spyglasses on Sally's house. Sally's signal was the
shades being down at night and up in the morning. As
Granny trained her spyglass on Sally's house, she
remembered that Sally was no longer there. Granny put
her binoculars down and sank into her chair with her
glass of wine and a sob came out of her body. Tears
began to fall as Granny mourned for her friend.

The shysters and Baskerville hadn't left yet for their
nightly excursion and they didn't know what to make of
Granny sobbing in her chair. Granny never cried, this
was something new that they hadn't encountered since
they joined her household. Baskerville, big lug that he
was, tried to crawl into Granny's lap. Both Furball and
Fish started licking her cheeks. Tank and Little White
Poodle dragged a blanket from the couch and covered
her feet. All of the attention from the shysters and
especially Baskerville trying to crawl into her lap
almost tipped Granny over in the chair. As she caught
herself she started laughing instead of crying.

Granny stood up. She remembered parts of
Ecclesiastes 3:4. What were some of those words? *A
time to be born and a time to die, a time to weep and a
time to laugh, a time to mourn and a time to dance.*
Granny guessed this was one of those times. Sally was
dead. Granny had done her weeping and would mourn
but Sally would want the grass to still keep talking and
others to still keep living. Sally would want Granny to
laugh and dance. Granny would do that but...she sure

as heck was going to get Sally's killer while she was dancing and laughing.

Granny skipped to her bedroom, said good night to the shysters and Baskerville as they would be leaving soon on their nightly routine ending up at Franklin's house before retracing their daily routines and ending up back at Granny's house. She put on her purple leather pj's that stated *Sexy Granny and I Know It* and plopped into bed.

Granny was deep asleep and dreaming about shopping at Red Hot Momma's Boutique. She was trying on a new sequined bra when a loud howl brought her straight up in bed, her heart pounding. She grabbed the knitting needle that she had taken from Sally's house that she had thrown on the floor earlier in the day. It still held the note Franklin had skewered. Granny slipped into her flip flops, held the knitting needle in front of her. She knew she should bring her umbrella to bed so she had a weapon in the middle of the night if she needed it but the knitting needle would have to do.

Granny started her swat team shuffle across the floor, all the while the howling kept rising. Granny opened the door and stuck the knitting needle through the crack. She then put one eye to the crack of the door and peered through. There was nothing in the hallway. Quietly and carefully she shuffled down the hall, hopping left to right to fend off any intruder. When she got to the living room and kitchen, the only occupant in the room besides Granny was Baskerville howling at the door. It appeared the Shysters had left on their nightly journey and Baskerville, after getting stuck one time too many in the door wasn't going to risk trying to sneak through it again. Granny put down the knitting needle, unlocked the door and let Baskerville out. She was going to have to figure out a way for Baskerville to get in and out so he didn't get stuck and he didn't interrupt her beauty sleep.

Granny shut the door, turned the lock and, still holding the knitting needle, grabbed her umbrella that was sitting by the door. Slowly she started shuffling back to her room in her flip flops so she wouldn't do the flip flop and prove her children right. As she was about to set the knitting needle down by her bedside, she lifted it up and stared at it intently. A smile crossed her face; she shook her head before putting the knitting needle down, crawling into bed with a smug look on her face.

CHAPTER NINE

Granny opened one eye slowly. It was enough to see that it was daylight out. Granny wiggled a little, closed her one open eye and snuggled back into her soft bed. Usually if Granny saw that the sun was up she would open the other eye very slowly, not wanting to get too excited to start the day. Getting up too fast always made Granny's head spin and it was already spinning from all the excitement of the past few days.

Normally, Granny would stick her big toe out of the blanket to determine the weather. Her big toe was a good barometer. If it started turning blue she knew it was cold and her toe was going to throb on and off throughout the day. If it was red, Granny knew it was a good day for her flip flops.

However, on this day, as Granny settled back into her mattress deciding to delay checking her big toe until later, she was startled awake at loud barking, hissing and thunking.

What in the world?

Granny jumped out of bed, grabbed the bedpost to keep herself from spinning onto the floor, grabbed both her umbrella, which was sitting by the bed, and the knitting needle, forgetting to put anything on her feet and also forgetting she had on her purple leather pj's as she dashed down the hall toward the noise.

Granny's pounding heart slowed down as she saw that the four shysters were trying to get the door open by jumping at the locks and the handle. The racket must have been them communicating to each other trying to figure out the problem, although Granny didn't know if meows and hisses could understand barking and growling and visa versa. The shysters were back from their nightly excursion and were trying to get Baskerville back in the house.

"I will fix this problem if I have to sledge hammer a bigger hole out of my door. I need my beauty sleep!" Granny exclaimed loudly to the shysters as she unlocked the locks and flung open the door. Her eyes opened wider at the sight of George and Mavis standing on the other side of the door along with Baskerville.

George and Mavis' eyes were wide in astonishment as they saw Granny's attire. Granny, remembering what she was wearing, slammed the door shut before Baskerville could get in. Baskerville uttered a loud, anguished howl.

"What do you want?"

"We heard the commotion," said George, "and since you always check on us we thought we had better return the favor and check on you to make sure you hadn't danced the last dance."

"I'm still dancing, thank you." Granny replied through the door.

"We can see that," Mavis answered with a smirky lilt in her voice. "Is the name of the dance, 'I'm sexy and I know it?'"

Granny ignored the teasing tone. "You can go now. I'll make sure I save the last dance until much later in my life, say 100 years. I'll let you know when my dance card is full."

"One more thing; we heard Sally's funeral is tomorrow. Thought you'd want to know. Oh," George continued, hollering as he and Mavis headed back down the sidewalk on the way to Mavis' house. "You might want to let Baskerville in, he's got a big steak in his mouth and it might need to be refrigerated."

Granny waited to open the door for Baskerville, watching out of her window to make sure Mavis and George were safely back at Mavis' house.

Granny opened the door and was trying to grab the steak out of Baskerville's mouth, wondering who he had stolen it from. It was common knowledge that the shysters were good at thieving. Now Baskerville had picked up their bad habits or he had learned them from his former owner. The theme from *Dragnet*, the '50's television hit started playing on her cell phone. *Dragnet* was the ring Granny had assigned to Franklin, since he was a former New York City detective; she thought the ring suited him.

It took Granny a minute to decide if she should let Baskerville win the steak or if she should answer Franklin's call. Curiosity won out.

"What?"

"Good Morning to you too, Hermiony, sweetheart."

"I'm not your sweetheart and it's Granny. Remember that; Granny."

"Hermiony, sweetheart, is that any way to talk to your fiancé?"

"What do you want, Franklin?"

"I think we need to talk; I have some news."

"What news?"

"I think we better talk in person. I'll be right over."

"No. I need to go to work. The merchants of Fuchsia are depending on me. I'll meet you at Ella's Enchanted Forest in a half hour." Granny slammed down the phone before Franklin could utter another word."

Granny hurried into her bedroom and dressed in her working Granny wardrobe. She tied her sparkly, high top tennis shoes, checked in the mirror to see that her hat was on crooked, fed Fish, the Little White Poodle, Furball and Tank, Baskerville already had the steak so she wasn't going to worry about his food. What was she going to do about Baskerville? She couldn't leave the door open. Granny picked up her umbrella tapping it on the ground as she thought.

"Baskerville, come with me."

Granny led Baskerville down the stairs, opened the fireplace door and left it open. She proceeded into the hidden room and opened the door to the underground streets.

"You'll have to use this door until I get it figured out, Baskerville." Baskerville gave a quiet howl before the two of them climbed back up the stairs to the front door.

"All of you, be good and no more stealing. Baskerville, no more steaks!!"

Granny started out the door with her umbrella in hand but turned back to pick up the knitting needle, sticking it in her large purse that was slung over her neck. Giving one more warning look to Fish, Little White Poodle, Furball, Tank and Baskerville, Granny closed the door and stood on the porch glancing over the neighborhood.

With a little sniff as she looked at Sally's house, Granny proceeded to the garage, hit the garage door opener ready to jump into one of her red '57 Chevy Corvettes parked in the garage.

Granny shut the garage door, deciding to walk uptown. Granny looked at the trees and saw the leaves were starting to turn. Fall was here. The grass was still green but soon the grass and the weeds would be covered with the cloak of the fallen leaves. As Granny turned to start her walk, she decided to take a detour through her back yard.

Granny sat down on the mound of grass that Sally had given her as a gift and Granny had used to bury the secrets she had tried to keep from the Big Guy. As Granny sat on the mound of grass and looked at the trees in her backyard, she could hear Sally saying to her, "The grass talks to you." When Granny had scoffed at her, Sally had replied, "All living things talk if you listen."

Granny fingered the grass knowing that soon it would be dormant. She listened to the whisper of the wind in the trees and the whisper of the falling leaves. Granny stroked the grass with light fingers. "I wish your grass would talk to me now, Sally, and tell me why you aren't here anymore. I wish it would talk to me and tell me who did this to you and why. You were the kindest soul on this earth. I never told you but I admired that about you." Granny took one more soft stroke of the grass, lowered her head and put her ear to the ground, patted the mound softly one time before using her umbrella to lift herself up for her walk into town.

Granny walked slowly, watching as the falling leaves made designs on the sidewalk in front of her. She was so busy studying the sidewalk and the leaves, making sure she didn't step on the cracks as she walked that she didn't see the big moving van blocking the sidewalk in front of Mrs. Shrill's house until her hat came in contact with the van and fell off of her head.

As Granny was rubbing the knot on her head from the bump, she stared up at the big truck. Lifting her umbrella she started pounding on the truck shouting, "Move it! Move it! Move it!"

She stopped when she felt a tug on her skirt. Granny looked down into the wide blue eyes of a little blonde haired girl. The girl was holding Granny's hat. "Who are you and why are you hitting the truck?"

Granny stopped hitting the moving van. "Who are you and where did you come from?"

"My name is Angelique but you can call me Angel like my mommy does. I live here now."

Granny bent down even with the little girl and took her hat. "My name is Granny and you can call me Granny. I live a couple of blocks away."

"I can't call you Granny. I already have a Granny. But she lives far away."

Granny sat down on the ground next to the little girl called Angel.

"Well, then, you can call me Hermiony. But don't call me that when anyone else is around. Agreed?"

Angel shook her head up and down. "Agreed."

"How old are you, Angel?"

"I'm four. How old are you?"

Granny stood up quickly. "Don't have time to talk about that now. I have to go. Nice meeting you, Angel." Granny plopped her hat on top of her head, moved around the front of the moving truck and picked up her pace to get downtown before Franklin came looking for her.

CHAPTER TEN

Franklin was waiting for Granny as she entered Ella's. He had her latte and donuts waiting for her. Franklin stood and pulled out a chair for Granny.

Granny stood for a moment, taking in the scene. Suspiciously she eyed Franklin. "Let's make this quick, Franklin; I have to get to work." Granny was going to continue the protest about his pulling out her chair for her when she noticed the somber look on his face.

Granny plunked down in her chair uncharacteristically quiet. She took a sip of her latte as she waited for Franklin to say something.

Franklin cleared his throat. "There's something I have to tell you."

"You don't want to be my fiancé?" That's ok, Franklin. I was trying to throw my kids off track. If they thought you and I were an item, they might not make me live with them or send me to the wrinkle farm." Granny patted his hands and stood up to leave, grabbing her donut to eat on her rounds.

Franklin gently grabbed her arm and pulled her back down in her chair. "No, Granny, it's about Esmeralda Periwinkle."

Granny squinted her eyes, glaring at Franklin, waiting for him to finish

"She's dead; they found her this morning in her chair, teacup in her lap."

Delight and her daughter Ella were standing behind the counter, waiting for Granny's reaction. The news of Granny's little episode at Mrs. Periwinkles had been whispered around town the evening before, and the news of Esmeralda Periwinkle's death coming on top of Granny's meltdown turned the little flame of news into a wildfire of speculation.

Granny stood up so fast that her chair fell and slid across the floor almost knocking over Ditty Belle from Persnickity's Bookstore as she came in the door for her morning coffee.

Granny picked up her umbrella and pointed it at Franklin's chest. "This is your fault, Franklin Jester Gatsby. I told you that she was going to die but you didn't believe me. This is on you, do you understand?" Granny turned and stomped out of Ella's, drawing everyone's attention.

Franklin sat back down and grabbed Granny's unfinished donut. "More donuts, Delight, and keep them coming."

"Um...are you sure it's donuts you want and not a stiff drink? I know Granny could drive you to drink, but drive you to donuts?" Delight asked perplexed at the order.

"No, Ella, I meant donuts. Maybe if I eat like Granny and drink like Granny, I'll understand Granny and she won't drive me so crazy."

As Franklin scarfed down donuts Granny checked out Pickles Grocery Store to see if there were any beady eyed ruffians trying to get away with any goods. She happened to be walking around the corner of the cooler by the milk when she noticed a puddle of milk on the floor. There seemed to be a path of drips leading down the aisle to the baked goods. Sure enough, there was Tricky Travis Trawler reaching for an open box of brownies. It was strange since Travis usually limited his pilfering to the collection plate at church but there was no doubt it was Travis stuffing his pockets with brownies, and milk was dripping out of his pockets.

Granny moved closer, hobbling slowly with her umbrella, her purse hanging from around her neck. With her free hand, Granny reached her hand into her purse and pulled out the knitting needle. She moved closer, brushing by Travis. As she was even with the pockets in his jacket, she took a couple of quick jabs at the pocket and quickly put the knitting needle back in her purse, but not before she was sure the boxes of milk and Travis had experienced the end of her knitting needle. As Travis jumped and howled at the point of the needle skewering the box and hitting his skin, Granny hit the remote alarm to alert the Big Guy. Granny then threw herself on the floor in the dripping milk puddle knocking Travis off his feet as he came down from hopping from the jabs.

At this point, the Big Guy swooped in. "What's the trouble?"

"I slipped on the milk that seems to be dripping out of Travis' pocket."

"You jabbed me. You skewered me."

"Young man, I did no such thing. I was passing by, minding my own business when I slipped on the milk that seemed to be pouring out of your pocket as you were hopping up and down for some odd reason."

"Search her. She skewered me with something. I have the marks to prove it."

"Granny, I have to check you out. Open your purse." The Big Guy gave Granny a hand and helped her to her feet.

The big guy slyly winked at Granny. Granny winked back.

"If you must, but isn't it strange that there is milk dripping out of one of his pockets and his other pocket seems to be muddy." Granny then took her hand and hit Travis other pocket and squashed all the brownies he had stowed in it. Granny opened her purse.

"Sorry, Travis, nothing sharp in there. You better empty your pockets. I'll take care of this now, Granny."

"If you say so, Big Guy." Granny winked and limped down the aisle and to the side of the store to visit the ladies' room. Once inside, she lifted her skirt and pulled the knitting needle out of her stocking that was held up on her thigh by elastic the old fashioned way. This made a good hiding place in a pinch and as Granny had landed on the floor she quickly had lifted the side of her skirt closest to the shelves and slipped the knitting needle out of her purse into the leg of her hose before Travis had noticed.

After Granny made sure that things were quiet, she walked down the way to LuLu's Quilt Shop. As Granny walked in the door, the door chimes started playing "Silver Threads and Golden Needles" to alert Lulu that she had a customer. For some reason, LuLu adopted the song for her quilt shop claiming she liked silver thread and golden needles even though the song didn't have anything to do with quilting. But that was the way it was in Fuchsia. People could have their unique likes and quirky habits. That is what set Fuchsia apart from other communities.

"Hi, Granny, what can I do for you?"

"Do you know how to knit?"

"Granny, this is a quilt shop but I do knit for a hobby. Did you want to learn?"

"No, I need to know where I can get a special knitting needle made."

"I do know of an online business that does that. You have to give them your specifications; they will make it and send it to you. Do you want me to look it up on the computer and see if we can order you something?"

"I do but this is secrecy at its highest level, Lulu. Can I trust you?"

"Are you going to get in trouble with this?"

Granny crossed her fingers behind her back. "No."

"Will I get into trouble for doing this?"

Again Granny crossed her fingers behind her back. "I promise no."

"Would your kids approve?"

This time Granny didn't have to cross her fingers. "No."

"Then let's do it."

CHAPTER ELEVEN

Granny was in the middle of her usual dream with the Mayor presenting her with a key to the city of Fuchsia when the phone's jarring ring woke her right as the key was in her grasp. As she started reaching for the phone, her doorbell started dinging and dinging and dinging. Who on earth would have the nerve to bother her at this time of the morning?

Granny held the phone to her ear as she reached under her bed for her white chenille robe to cover her Fuchsia nightie that was lined with purple and pink fur.

"What?" Granny shouted into the phone.

"Granny, this is Mayor Horatio Helicourt."

Granny held the phone out to look at the receiver. She pinched herself to make sure she wasn't still asleep and dreaming.

"Yes?"

"Granny, we are having a ceremony on Thursday afternoon at Ella's Enchanted Forest and we would like you to be there."

"Are you sure you have the right number and the right Granny?"

"I am sure; the ceremony starts at 2:00 p.m. sharp."

"I haven't done anything wrong. I am an old lady and you need to tell me what this is about."

"Just be there and ah...bring your critters along with you."

"My critters?"

"You know—the dogs and cats that live with you that always seem to be in trouble."

Granny was about to ask another question when Horatio Helicourt hung up the phone. It took Granny a minute to realize the doorbell was still ringing in her ear. Muttering to herself about this new dilemma of being summoned by the Mayor, she shuffled down the hallway and threw open the door.

"Granny, why didn't you answer the door? Couldn't you hear us? Maybe you need hearing aids. At your age, the hearing goes you know." George and Mavis stood hand in hand on Granny's porch.

"I can hear just fine, thank you. I was just getting my binoculars ready to check on you and make sure you were ok. I'm the one who is supposed to check on you if you remember. Maybe your memories are a little foggy," Granny shot back.

She started shutting the door when George stuck his foot out and blocked Granny from closing the door. Granny gave him the eagle eye.

"We have news."

At those words, Granny held the door open and let them in, making sure her white chenille robe was tightly wrapped around her body so nothing underneath was revealed. She didn't want her neighbors to think she was a night party animal.

"I hope it's news about Sally's murderer. I have been trying to sneak into her yard and her house but every time I get close, the Big Guy seems to appear out of nowhere. You don't suppose he's watching me do you? I'll have him arrested for harassment."

"Granny, he's the one who does the arresting."

"Well, haven't you heard of a citizen's arrest? I'm a citizen."

"Can we sit down?" Mavis moved toward the couch, grabbing George's hand, drawing him along with her."

As Granny was about to question them further, the doorbell rang again.

"Doesn't anyone ever sleep in on Wednesday morning?" Granny shouted as she opened the door to the wide-eyed stare of Legs—as Granny called him because he had such cute legs—her UPS Driver.

"What are you doing here so early in the morning?"

"Ah, it's noon," Legs stammered. "I have this package for you." He handed Granny a three foot long narrow package.

"Noon; I never sleep till noon. Your clock's off, but thanks for the package." Granny shut the door and quickly stashed the package in the closet behind the door.

"Looks interesting, Granny,." Mavis asked with curiosity.

"Now, what's this all about?" Granny asked, ignoring Mavis' comment. "I haven't seen much of you since Sally's funeral two weeks ago except in your window."

"That's what we came to tell you, Granny." Mavis snuck a quick look at George. "We're moving in together."

George took Mavis' hand and looked at Granny with what Granny considered a dopey look. "I'm renting my house out. At our ages we want to be sure. We're not getting any younger as you should know, Granny."

"You're getting hitched?"

"No, NO! Nothing like that!" George answered in a loud voice.

Mavis clarified their statement. "We are sharing expenses like two later in years adults."

"You mean *old*, don't you?" Granny cracked in her most snickery voice.

"We'll see where it leads," Mavis piped in as she looked adoringly at George.

"Straight to the wrinkle farm when your kids find out." At that statement, Granny walked over and held open the door. "I know the news, your house is for rent, you're sharing expenses and I have a crime to solve. It's been two weeks since Sally and Mrs. Periwinkle were murdered and I need to find out why."

"That was nice touch at her funeral, Granny, to dig up a little of the grass Sally gave you and put it on her casket. I am sure Sally is talking to the grass from heaven." Mavis gave a little sniffle as she walked out the door followed by George.

Granny peeked through her window shades to make sure they were gone. The shysters were nowhere to be seen so Granny figured they must still be out scavenging. She shook her head, looking at the clock on the microwave in the kitchen, wondering how she had slept so late. Granny grabbed her donut, a cup of the coffee, now cold, since the timer was set to go off at 8:00 a.m. and only kept the coffee warm for an hour. She popped the coffee into the microwave for a quick warm-up (Granny hated microwave coffee but she was craving her coffee fix). Then, she proceeded to the closet to retrieve the package that Lulu had ordered for her two weeks ago. Granny was impressed that it had gotten here this soon as it had to be made especially for her.

As Granny sipped her warmed up coffee and nibbled on her donut, she opened her package wondering why she hadn't heard from her kids in a couple of weeks. Yes, they had made the occasional phone call to check up on her but there had been no visits. Even with the phone calls there had been no more talk of the wrinkle farm. Perhaps introducing Franklin as her fiancé had taken care of the situation. Although it might be tricky keeping up the pretense if her children visited again, since Franklin still had his shorts in a knot over their last encounter at Ella's a couple of weeks ago before Sally's funeral. She hadn't heard from him since.

Granny held up the new custom-built cane that she had ordered. It was an aluminum cane, rounded and bright pink, you might almost call it Fuschia (or was it Fuchsia like the name of their community?). Granny never could remember the spelling even as long as she had lived here. Was it *s* before *c,* and before or after *h*?. Granny shook her head thinking about it, such a confusing name, which was perfect for her community. On the end of the cane was a rubber flat bottom that gave it good stability for her to lean on if she needed it. It was her new weapon of choice to protect the community of Fuchsia.

Granny put the cane aside to get herself ready for her journey uptown. Looking out the window, she knew it was not a flip flop day even if she hadn't had time to check her big toe that morning. She knew it was a little on the blue side. Fall had arrived.

As Granny was ready to walk out the door, she remembered she needed to figure out something so Baskerville could have a front door way into the house. She studied the side window by the door. It was long and tall and wide, enough room for him to get through. Granny touched the window with her fingers, running them along side of the casing. All of a sudden, Granny's eyes got wide; she stood up straight and with the determination of a woman on a mission; she bounded out the front door carrying her pocketbook and her new cane.

CHAPTER TWELVE

Granny glanced at the houses across the street as she started her walk. The weeds were still surrounding Sally's house, although they were starting to turn a little brown with the fall weather, but weeds always seemed to last longer than grass in the fall. The police tape must have been taken down during the night. Granny made a note to check out Sally's house later when she came back home.

George and Mavis waved at her from Mavis' front window. George seemed to be caught up now in Mavis' fantasies as they were both wearing wide-brimmed hats and toasting with cups of what looked like tea cups. Granny hoped it wasn't lavender tea but she knew Mavis had a green tea thing going in the morning, claiming it was healthy.

Granny glanced at George's house and wondered if he had found a renter. As she made her way to Main Street, she stopped in front of what had once been Mrs. Shrill's house. A hopscotch board had been drawn on the sidewalk in chalk. Granny looked around to see if anyone was looking. Setting her pocketbook and new cane down on the ground, she took a leap and started jumping on the hopscotch squares when she heard a tiny voice.

"Why do you have the cane if you can jump like that, Hermiony?"

Granny looked around to see Angelique watching her. Granny stopped jumping and reached down for her cane and pocketbook before gesturing Angelique over to her.

"I need my cane to walk, see?" Granny demonstrated her walk with the cane. "But I don't need my cane to jump. My legs have hinges in them. I would show you but my hose covers my legs and ladies don't take their hose down in public. Let's not tell anyone about this, ok?"

"My Mommy and my Grandpa said I'm not supposed to keep secrets."

Granny looked down at Angelique. "Of course not, of course not. They are right. What about us pretending I wasn't here. If they ask you, tell them the truth but since they don't know I was here, they probably won't ask."

"You make me mixed up. My Grandpa does that sometimes too. I guess that happens when you get old. Where's the hose? I don't see a hose?" Angel looked closely at Granny's legs as she rambled on not waiting for an answer. "Do you have a dog? I want a dog. My grandpa has a dog and a cat but my mommy says I can't have a dog or a cat cause Grandpa's dog and cat get in too much trouble. Bye, I got to go now; my mommy is taking me to stay with my Grandpa today." Angelique skipped off just as fast as she had appeared.

Granny wondered about Angelique's mom and grandpa. She'd have to investigate that later. Granny hurried on. She had to get her plan for Baskerville's door in motion.

When Granny got to the main street of Fuchsia, she noticed that the street department had been busy putting up the pumpkin lights that decorated the lampposts during the Halloween and Thanksgiving season. They stayed up past Halloween, and dangling lighted turkeys were added until Thanksgiving when the Christmas lights were put up. On Halloween, the Giant Pumpkin visited and was plunked down in the middle of Rack's parking lot. It was a giant inflatable pumpkin that was hollow inside so kids could visit the inside and jump and tumble until their hearts were content. Granny thought her new friend Angelique would love the lights and the pumpkins.

As Granny passed Abstract and Ella's Enchanted Forest and Pickle's Grocery, she took a gander in the windows to make sure she didn't see anything suspicious. She didn't have time for those pesky beady eyed shop-lifting crooks today, she was on a mission. She passed the Wrench Bench in front of Nail's Hardware store and opened the front door listening to the jingling of the nail wind chimes that Mr. Nail had made to alert him when a customer was present.

"Hi, Granny, business is slow today, not many customers. I can keep an eye on them if you have somewhere else where they need your snoopy eyes more."

"My eyes are not snoopy, and, besides, that's what you pay me for, to snoop!" Granny answered in an argumentative tone.

"Calm down, Granny; it was just a figure of speech."

"I need your son Neil. He's a carpenter, right? And a computer whiz? I need both."

"He's not here right now but he'll be back soon. I can send him over to your house when he gets back."

"Tell Neil that I will meet him at Ella's Enchanted Forest. I need some of that Boneyard Coffee that they serve there. Kind of fits with the theme of the next holiday, Halloween; get it? Boneyard?" Granny gave a laugh, nudged Mr. Nail with her pocketbook and walked out the door leaving Mr. Nail shaking his head at Granny's strange sense of humor.

Ella's Enchanted Forest seemed to be empty except for a couple of town council members examining the

Forest Room. As Granny sat down, she looked around, hoping Franklin was somewhere hidden in a corner.

"Hi, Granny, What would you like today? Want to try our new Boneyard Specialty coffee? The flavor of the day is Boneyard Blend. It's a coffee roasted at Boneyard Coffee & Tea in Champaign, Illinois.

"Hi, Delight, That's what I came for. I got your email announcing you were serving it. Wonderful thing, this high falutin' technology; solves many a problem for me even if I don't use it much. I'll have a chocolate donut stuffed with cream cheese, drizzled with chocolate and topped with whipped cream and a cup of that Boneyard Blend Specialty coffee. Have you seen Franklin?"

"Not since that day a few weeks ago after Sally and Mrs. Periwinkle died and you and Franklin were having that little chat here. You left and he kept eating donut upon donut. He ate so many donuts I ran out."

"Franklin eating donuts?"

Just at that moment, Neil Nail walked in the door and made a beeline for Granny.

"Hey, Granny; what's up?"

"Apparently not your pants. Pull those pants up where they belong. Your boxers are too much for this old ladies heart. The only boxers I want to see are the dog kind and George's hanging from his pole in the morning." Granny took the round handle of her new cane and hitched it under Neil's waistband of his pants and tugged upward with enough strength that Neil thought his feet might leave the ground.

"Ok, Granny, I got your point."

"I have a drawing and here's what I want you do." Granny handed the plans to Neil. Be at my house 8:00 a.m. sharp. I want it done before sundown tomorrow night. Got it?"

"These are quite the plans, Granny. Where did you learn about technology like this?"

"Search engine, son, search engine."

"Got it, see ya tomorrow."

"I'll see you too, hopefully not as much as I saw today. I don't want to give Mavis across the street any more ideas for her reality show and George might get jealous about your colorful boxers and you never know what might happen if you rile George up."

Watching Neil leave reminded Granny that maybe she should check on Franklin. Even Tank and Furball hadn't brought her anything from his house lately. After all, he was her fiancé so she should be worried about him.

As Granny was contemplating checking on Franklin, Delight sat down across from her.

"Do you see those town council guys over there?" Delight said in a whisper.

"Why are you whispering?" Granny whispered back.

"Because it's a secret."

"So why are you telling me?"

"Because you can keep a secret and besides you're forgetful so you may not remember it anyway and I have to tell someone before I burst."

Granny took a swig of coffee and finished off a donut. She leaned forward, took Delight's hand in hers, looked her straight in the eyes and said, "You can tell me anything, Delight. Your secret is safe with me." And then she winked at Delight to reassure her that she was telling the truth.

"My forest room is going to become Graves Mortuary. They are moving to my building."

Granny immediately pulled her hand away having an aversion to the mortuary business at least until she was 100 when the possibility of her needing their services might be a more comforting thought. "Have you gone daft? I don't want to have my lattes while Mr. or Mrs. Stiff are hanging around in the forest."

"That's the good part. We are trading buildings. The city has offered me Graves' old building completely renovated in the shape of a teapot and coffeepot. There is room next to the building to add my Forest and add on an enclosed sunroom in the shape of a donut with patio seating in the summer time. It's a win-win situation. But you can't tell anyone. It's not official yet."

Granny reached out and touched Delight's forehead. "You do feel a little warm; are you sure you are not dreaming this? Why would the city do that?"

"Because it's Fuchsia and they are always doing unusual things and what fits in more with the community than a building shaped like a coffeepot and teapot? They are going to reveal the news on Thursday at 2:00 p.m. at a press conference in the Forest Room."

"I got a phone call this morning that I am supposed to be in the Forest Room to meet the Mayor the same day and time the press conference is going on. I thought I was in trouble. Why would I need to be there?"

"Not a word, Granny, not a word."

"Did you just say something to me, Delight? I forgot my hearing aid. See you." Granny picked up her cane and pocketbook, turned an eye on the two men in the forest room, shook her head and started for the door when she tripped on her cane. As Granny was going down, two arms caught her and lifted her off of the floor. She looked down straight into the eyes of Franklin Jester Gatsby.

"Falling for me again, Granny. I thought we had gotten past that." Granny blushed before steadying herself with her cane when he set her back down on the ground.

"Where have you been, Franklin Jester Gatsby?"

"Investigating murders, Granny. I have now joined the Fuchsia Police Department as an investigator part time, at least for the investigation into Sally and Mrs. Periwinkle's murders."

"And you didn't tell me, your own fiancé!" Granny stomped her cane on the floor for emphasis.

"Nothing to tell, Granny, nothing to tell."

"You don't have clues? You don't have suspects? And why have you been staying away from me? I could help you."

"A few clues but none I can talk about. No suspects. I can't think straight when I'm with you and you have gotten yourself in enough trouble lately. I am saving you from yourself. If you get yourself in anymore scrapes, it'll be the wrinkle farm for you for sure if your kids have their way."

"Ah," Granny said dismissively, "I haven't heard from them for weeks either." Granny looked at him suspiciously. "Are you teaming up with them, Franklin? Is there something I don't know?" Granny thought Franklin was looking a little sheepish. Right away she was on her guard. "Got to go, got an early morning appointment and I've got to talk to the shysters. They should be home by now. Bye." Granny slammed the door loudly behind her.

"My Grandpa says it's rude to slam doors?"

Granny almost tripped over the little blue-eyed angel who was aptly name Angelique before bumping into an older version of Angelique. The older version of Angelique was as pretty and as tiny as what Granny guessed to be her daughter.

The woman looked at Granny with a speculative look.

Granny gave in and bent down to the little girl. "I wasn't really slamming the door, the wind caught it and slammed it shut."

"But there's no wind," Angel, as she wanted to be called, innocently informed Granny.

"Well, um, ah, maybe I was mistaken and did accidently slam the door. I, ah, um, will um, try to, ah, maybe not do it again?" Granny said in a cajoling tone.

"My name's Heather," the older version of Angel introduced herself as she held out her hand.

"Granny." Granny stuck out her hand while eyeing Angel, wondering if she was going to give away her real name. Angel was more interested in looking at the cupcakes in the window. "I met your little girl when my hat bumped into your moving truck as I was walking downtown. You must excuse me; I am expecting to be followed and I have to go" Granny looked back over her shoulder to make sure Franklin wasn't trying to pursue her. When she didn't see him she continued on her way home.

CHAPTER THIRTEEN

Granny woke with a start the next morning. She had been dreaming that she was walking down the aisle with Franklin and just as they were about to say, "I do," the mayor of Fuchsia popped up and interrupted the wedding by trying to give her a key to the city. Just as he was about to hand her the key in place of the wedding ring that Franklin had been going to place on her finger, the racket had started and woke her up.

Granny hopped out of bed and landed in her swat team pose unthinkingly before she realized it was someone pounding on her front door and ringing her door bell at the same time. It was a good thing she had slept in her clothes last night. After her glass of wine and a marathon of *The Old and the Hopeless* soap opera she had been too tired to even take off her glasses before she tumbled into bed. Holding in a few choice words that she never said in front of her children even when they weren't there, she proceeded down the hallway and into the living room, threw open the front door ready to skewer whoever it was with her raised eyebrow Granny look, until she realized it was Neil Nail.

"Forgot I was coming, didn't ya, Granny? Bright and early you said."

"It's 6:00 a.m., bright and early is 8:00 a.m. in Fuchsia."

"I'm bright and I'm early. The early bird catches the worm, you know."

"Or the snake," Granny said with a smirk. "I'm going across the street while you work. The shysters are gone already. You know what you have to do. And remember, my eyes will still be on you from afar." Granny turned and picked up her binoculars, her new cane and walked out the door, leaving Neil Nail to figure out the plans Granny had left with him yesterday.

Granny decided this was a good time to scope out Sally's house. It was too early for anyone to be watching her. The street seemed deserted as she strolled across the street lifting her binoculars to peer into Mavis' house to see if she could see any signs of life this early in the morning. George's house was sitting empty and Granny missed the surprise of whatever color of boxer shorts he hung on the pole in the morning.

Granny turned around to look at her house and she could see Neil busy with her project. He wasn't watching. Granny walked up the steps and tried the door, locked tight. She took a bobby pin from her hair and straightened it out and threaded it into the lock. She jimmied it and turned it and shook it and twisted it, but, no luck; she couldn't open this lock.

Granny checked each basement window. They were locked tight too. Using her binoculars she put them up to the window to see if she could see anything out of the ordinary in the basement. It was empty. Had someone cleaned out Sally's basement when Granny wasn't looking? Or had it been empty already? Granny hadn't been in Sally's basement for a long time.

Maybe there was a ladder in the garage. Granny tromped through the brown and drying weeds. The leaves were covering the ground and the trees were almost bare. Granny tried the garage door. Locked. She tried her bobby pin. It wouldn't even go into the lock. What kind of locks were these that she couldn't get a bobby pin in? Granny hopped up to see if she could see anything in the windows? If anyone saw her she would look like a kid on a pogo stick.

Granny gave up and sat down on the ground. Maybe there was a clue out here? Granny stood up and took her bright pink new cane and started threading through the weeds inch by inch. Every once in a while she looked up to see if anyone was watching. Granny didn't know how long she had been searching for the elusive mystery object of which she didn't know what it was, when she heard a swish behind her. George and Mavis were now in the yard with her and they each had a rake in their hand.

"If you tell us what you lost, Granny, we will help you look for it." Mavis whispered.

"We saw you looking and thought we would help. It's a big lawn. What did you drop?" George asked.

Granny raised her cane in mid-air and paused, "My teeth." Granny covered her mouth and looked down so they wouldn't see that her teeth were still in her mouth. I dropped my teeth when I was chasing the shysters." Granny quickly swished the weeds. "Look, I found them." Granny quickly bent down, rubbed her hand over her mouth as if putting in her teeth and stood up. Just at that moment they all heard a loud noise.

"Granny! Granny!"

"Granny! Granny!"

"That sounds like Neil Nail." Granny stood a little taller trying to listen.

A loud howl echoed over the neighborhood.

"That sounds like Baskerville." George and Mavis chimed in together. They all took off in a slow hop, run, hop, walk, run, out of Sally's back yard heading toward Granny's house. That was all their bodies would allow them to do.

Neil Nail was standing by the long narrow window next to Granny's front door. Baskerville was howling and the window was popping open. Neil would shut it, Baskerville would howl again and the window, now a door, would open again. Standing in the street next to his black '57 Chevy convertible was Franklin accompanied by Fish, Little White Poodle, Furball and Tank. Little White Poodle and Tank were barking their distinct barks. Fish and Furball were meowing in their loudest, "I found a mouse", meows. Franklin was leaning on his car as if nothing was happening.

"I'm here, Neil; what's wrong?" Granny gave a side glance at Franklin before hurrying up the steps.

"It's all done. I was testing it with Baskerville. Howl, Baskerville, howl!"

Baskerville let out his loudest howl, the newly made door, made out of the side window next to the real door, opened. Baskerville trotted in the house and the door closed. Fish, Little White Poodle, Furball and Tank hurried up the steps and ran into the house through their normal pet door.

Granny grinned, turned around and saw the scowl on Franklin's face and wondered what she had done now. She couldn't remember doing anything that Franklin might actually know about. Of course, he had seen her coming from Sally's place but she was with Mavis and George so he should surmise they were just having a chat. She didn't think she had forgotten that she had done anything that the Big Guy might have reported to Franklin so she wasn't quite sure what the scowl was about. And why were the shysters home so early?

"I'll be down to pay you later, Neil. I need to check out some fertilizer you might carry."

Neil looked at Granny and looked at Franklin. He hesitated for a moment, not sure if he should leave.

"Now, Neal." Granny tapped him lightly with her cane. Neal packed up his tools and took off down the steps.

Granny followed, deciding she might as well find out what she had forgotten she had done.

"Do you have a problem Franklin? Why are you here? Do you know why the shysters came home early?"

Franklin pulled himself up from leaning against his car.

Granny eyed him as he did that, thinking he was a tall, handsome man and occasionally she would admit her heart beat a little faster when she was with him. Maybe she should keep him as her fiancé. Or maybe her heart was beating a little faster from being worried about what she had forgotten she had done that put a scowl like this on his face.

"Your Fish and Little White Poodle are bad influences on my Itsy and Bitsy. I just bailed them all out of the hoosegow. Baskerville got away before they could catch him.:

"Who are Itsy and Bitsy? I don't believe I know them. All I see are Furball and Tank. What kind of trouble did Fish, Little White Poodle, Furball and Tank get into that would land them in the hoosegow and how did they know to call you?"

"Little White Poodle and Tank were digging a hole through the weeds in Mrs. Periwinkle's back yard. Fish and Furball were trying to scratch their way through the side screen door of the garage. The realtor caught them and called Wesley Weimeraner, the animal control officer. They knew to call me because unlike some people whose name I won't mention, I have Itsy and Bitsy equipped with a microchip."

"Why would they try and dig up her yard? If they want to dig up weeds all they have to do is run across the street?" Granny became thoughtful. "We have to go to Mrs. Periwinkle's, they must have found a clue and they wanted to bring it to me." Granny started heading toward her garage.

"I am not getting caught up in your harebrained schemes again, Hermiony. You need to stick to cornering your shoplifting, conniving crooks in the stores of Fuchsia and let the Big Guy and the Fuchsia Police Department handle this. The only reason I agreed to help them was to keep an eye on you and keep you from getting into trouble. Last time you almost got yourself killed."

"You can't tell me what to do, Franklin." Granny stomped her pink aluminum cane down on the ground to emphasize her words. "You are only my pretend fiancé." Granny turned, walked to her garage and with a flair of drama queen, made a wide sweep with her arm to the doorknob of the garage, opened the door, punched the garage door opener, continued to the first red '57 Corvette convertible sitting near the door and got in. She turned the key she had left in the car so she remembered where she had left her keys, revved the engine twice, backed out of the garage, turned the wheel to the right, came to a halt and hit the pedal squealing as she peeled down the road, waving at Franklin as he stood glaring at her from her front lawn.

CHAPTER FOURTEEN

Granny headed straight to Mrs. Periwinkle's house. She needed to see the hole the shysters had started digging and to check the garage to see what Fish and Furball were trying to get to. Instead of turning into Mrs. Periwinkle's driveway, she turned in Rack's parking lot. Neil Nail was walking in the front door of Mrs. Periwinkle's house with the realtor. Granny sat for a few minutes trying to decide whether to go into Rack's and sit in her favorite booth so she could watch what was happing at Mrs. Periwinkle's or give it up for the day.

Neil and the realtor seemed to be examining the entire property. Granny decided she would take the day off and head out of town to Brilliant, Minnesota, to Red Hot Momma's Boutique for an afternoon of shopping. Winter was coming soon and perhaps a little warmer attire might be in order for the colder months. She had donated last year's winter pj's anonymously to the Humane Society to auction off at their annual fundraiser.

Granny spent the afternoon adding to her winter nighttime wardrobe. She picked up a red, brushed velour, long-sleeved nightgown trimmed with black, sparkling beading and feathers around the edges of the cuffs and the bottom of the gown. Embroidered across the front were the words, "Sizzling and Saucy." She also found a pair of long-sleeved, hot pink silk pj's that buttoned down the front. The buttons weren't the ordinary buttons but red rhinestone heart buttons.

Rhinestone hearts also decorated the legs of the pj's moving in a line up the outsides of the legs to the heart-shaped openings right over the hips. The openings were lined with see through sheer fabric.

As Granny drove back into her neighborhood, she stopped the car dead at the end of her street. There was a moving truck at George's house and someone was moving in. There was also a moving truck at Sally's house and someone was moving in. How could that be? Sally had only been dead a couple of weeks and there hadn't even been a *for sale* sign on the house. George must have found a renter. That was fast work on his part too.

Granny continued into her garage and made a bee line for her house. As soon as she got inside, she grabbed her binoculars and started scoping out the two moving vans. All she could see at either place were the movers. The people moving in didn't seem to be there. Granny picked up the phone to call Mavis. The phone rang and rang but no one picked up, which Granny thought was strange since their cars were sitting in the driveway. Maybe they were involved in one of their fantasy reality shows and didn't hear the phone. Granny gave up after the 20th ring. It appeared their answering machine was off too.

Granny finally gave up the thought that she was going to see anything and put down her binoculars. It had been a long day. The shysters seemed to have left early. Granny walked downstairs and closed the secret door to the underground street and the fireplace door since Baskerville didn't need it anymore.

Once back in the kitchen, she checked the bowls to make sure Fish, Little White Poodle, Furball and Tank had eaten the yogurt and vegetables she had given them for breakfast. Then Granny pulled out her ice cream and donuts. She always seemed to think better when ice cream and donuts were sitting in front of her. She lifted her cane to examine it. It seemed to be working well for a undercover cane. No one suspected. Granny lifted the cane and took it and the ice cream and donuts into her bedroom. She was going to turn in early with a good book. Maybe she could learn something from one of those cozy detective mysteries. Granny picked up her newest book by Amy Beth Arkawy. It was an Eliza Gordon mystery called *Dead Silent*. Granny liked the name. It reminded her of Sally and Mrs. Periwinkle. They were pretty dead silent. Granny remembered Sally's last words. "The grass quit talking to me." The talking grass had been silent at the end of Sally's life too. With a sniff, Granny settled down in bed, wondering where the shysters had escaped to so early in the evening. She picked up the book and started to read. The words *dead silent* seemed to echo in her head. Why had the grass quit talking to Sally? Granny knew she had to figure it out.

Granny was right at the cliff hanger of the book, *Dead Silent*, when she was startled by the bang of the window door that Baskerville used and the sound of all of the shysters running through her house. She had left the bedroom door open and soon the padding of the paws ran into her room and under her bed. Granny thought perhaps she misnamed all of them. Their names should have been *flash* because that is all she caught of the sight of them before Fish, Little White Poodle, Tank and Furball, hightailed it under her bed. Baskerville headed for the closet but because the door was closed he slammed dead on into the closet door making a big racket. At the same time, the pounding and shouting started on her front door.

Granny quickly pulled up her new cane and took the end off of it to reveal a giant knitting needle with a sharp point at the end. Quickly moving down the hallway, she positioned herself by her front door. "Go away; I'm armed. I called the Big Guy."

"I'm not leaving until I deal with those menacing animals that ran into this house."

Granny looked down the hallway thinking that those animals didn't look too menacing now.

"Who are you? Go away before I use my weapon."

"Open this door before I call the police."

"Call the police? Call the police? You're attacking me!" With that Granny flung open the door and aimed her knitting needle at the intruder. Granny had to take a second look when she realized the loud voice came from a young woman in her early thirties who couldn't have weighed any more than Granny did, and she didn't have a weapon.

"Stand right there, young lady," Granny warned. "I've got you covered," Granny yelled as she held the giant knitting needle in front of her. "Who are you?"

"I'm Sally's daughter and I just moved in across the street and your marauding animals were trying to dig up my yard."

"My angels wouldn't dig in a pile of weeds and Sally didn't have a daughter. Don't move; I'm calling the Big Guy." The only problem was that the phone was in the bedroom and Granny was by the door and couldn't keep her weapon trained on the noisy intruder if she went to get her phone.

"Mom, what are you doing? What is that thing? It looks like a giant knitting needle. Put that pointy thing down. You might hurt someone," Thor instructed his mother as he strode up her sidewalk.

"What are you doing here at this time of night? This woman's trying to kill me and my furry children. Quick, call the police, Thor."

Thor walked up and took the giant knitting needle out of Granny's hands. He had to tug a little to get her to give it to him.

"Mom, this is Elena. Elena, this is my mother."

Granny turned to look at Thor and gave him her dagger look. Thor seemed unfazed. "She says she's Sally's daughter," said Granny. "Sally didn't have any daughters. How do you know her, Thor? And why are you here?"

"Yes," replied Thor. "Elena is Sally's daughter. They have been estranged for years. She just moved into Sally's house. I met her this afternoon, Mom. I checked with the Big Guy and she is who she says she is."

Granny turned the porch light on to peer more closely at Elena. "You don't look like Sally."

"I look like my grandmother on my father's side," Elena replied.

Granny raised her eyebrows in disbelief. "So why are you pounding on my door at this time of night?"

"Your pets were digging holes in my yard and they were scaring Gottlieb."

"Gottlieb? Who's Gottlieb?" Granny asked in confusion.

"He's my pet goat and he likes grazing on the weeds in my mother's yard, now my yard since I inherited the place."

"Well, you better go now; I'll talk to them." Granny pulled Thor into the house, stepped back and shut the door, leaving Elena staring at a closed door. Granny listened to Elena's steps retreating. Granny grabbed Thor's arm and led him over to the couch. She held up her hand to stop him from speaking and took the top off of the footstool by the chair in the corner. She lifted out the blankets and then gave a press on what looked like the bottom of the footstool. It popped up and out.

Granny took out two wine glasses and a bottle of wine. She poured a glass for Thor and handed it to him, then she proceeded to do the same for herself before she sat down next to Thor.

"Not a word to your sisters, do you understand? Or you will know what the giant knitting needle feels like."

Thor started laughing and held up his hands in front of him. "No problem, your secret is safe with me, Mom. Of course, it always has been because I have known about your secret stash for a long time. I am your son after all."

Granny peered at him through her glasses and gave him a disbelieving look. "Where did you come from and why are you here?"

"Nice nighttime attire, Mom."

Granny looked down. She had forgotten to check what she was wearing before she was rudely summoned from her bed by the floozy across the street. Granny was wearing her new nighttime attire that she had purchased at Red Hot Momma's Boutique. Luckily it was almost winter and although it was very colorful and adorned with sparklies, it wasn't too risqué and it covered her. Granny liked to be colorful but in the fall and winter, she liked to be warm. "Quit changing the subject!"

"I'm your new neighbor. I'm renting George's house."

Granny stood up so fast that she dropped her wine glass right in Thor's lap.

"I guess that's my cue to go." Thor laughed and stood up and sprinted for the door, turning around at the last second before he disappeared out the door. "Won't we have fun?"

Granny quickly ran to the window and peered through the blinds. Thor was going the wrong direction. He was going to Sally's house. Why would he go to

Sally's house? He certainly couldn't be going to see that floozy. And why was he living in George's house? Was that why her kids had let Granny stay here? And she had thought it was because she had introduced them to Franklin. As Granny peered out the window, she heard soft paw prints behind her. Then she heard a big slurp. Granny turned around just in time to see Baskerville slurping up the rest of Thor's wine, and Fish, the Little White Poodle, Furball and Tank heading for the door.

Granny sprinted over and blocked the doggy door but she wasn't quick enough to stop Baskerville from howling, opening his door and leaving, followed by the rest of the shysters. Granny walked to her bedroom and picked up her cellphone.

"Franklin, Granny here. I am breaking our engagement. And watch out for the shysters; they're on to something. I just know it." Granny walked back into the living room with her cell phone, set it on the table and turned it off for the night. She couldn't resist peeking out the blinds one more time. There were no lights on in George's old house or in Mavis' house, but there were lights in Sally's old house and Granny could see two figures through the window. Deep in thought, Granny plodded back to bed. After all, tomorrow she had to meet the mayor so she should get some beauty sleep. She would take care of Thor tomorrow.

CHAPTER FIFTEEN

Granny opened one eye slowly. She opened her second eye quickly. Her nose was picking up on something smoking and her ears were picking up on something sizzling. Granny sat up as fast she could and steadied herself with her bedpost. She slipped on her flip flops and clomped down the hallway as fast as she could run. Smoke seemed to be billowing down the hallway.

"Fire! fire! Someone help me!" Granny started yelling through the smoke. She grabbed a vase of stale water that she had left at the end of her hallway that still had dead flowers sitting in it and gave a toss toward the kitchen right into the face of Thor.

As Thor was trying to recover from the water in his face, Granny picked up the fish bowl that she used to have for her fish before they swam to the fishbowl in the sky, and tossed the water she still kept in the fish bowl in memory of her fish, at whatever was burning in the kitchen. This too landed in Thor's face as he was trying to stop her forward flight.!" Granny grabbed Thor and with her full 100 pound weight pushed him toward the door. "I don't want you to die trying to save me."

Thor turned, grabbed Granny and picked her up and set her down on a kitchen chair. "The bacon is burning, Mom; your house isn't on fire."

Granny looked at Thor, looked at the stove and looked around at the smoke in her house. "Why is there bacon burning on my stove?" Granny shouted. "I don't do bacon this early in the morning. I do donuts."

"I thought since I lived so close I would help you out a little bit, so I was making you breakfast."

"You don't know how to cook."

"I'm learning."

"You could have fooled me. I thought maybe you were trying out for the fire department. Why are you here? You didn't tell me you planned to make me breakfast last night."

"It's a nice change of scenery. My job ended. I have a stash put away so I can live comfortably for a while until I find a job. I thought I'd move here and help you out. Better me than my sisters or the wrinkle farm," Thor said in a cajoling voice. "Nice door for Baskerville, by the way."

Granny got up and stomped back to her room, stating, "Got to get dressed. I have a meeting with the mayor this afternoon and I am supposed to bring the shysters so I better round them up. Maybe I shouldn't bring them. Maybe it's a trick and the mayor wants to put the shysters in the doggie hoosegow. They have been getting into a little bit of trouble lately. On second thought, I think I'll forget the shysters and go down to Nail's Hardware and pay Neal Nail for his work yesterday. If you're good, you can meet me at Rack's for lunch."

"I already have plans. Rain check?" Thor winked at Granny and let himself out the front door.

Granny got herself dressed in her most respectable clothes. She put on her black, what she called her 'go to funeral' dress, threw on a matching black sweater and, instead of her granny hose, she put on her nylons and black patent flats. After all, she had to talk to the mayor and since she wasn't sure why he wanted to talk to her, she thought she had better dress the way people thought she should dress to look respectable. With a glint in her eye and a smile on her lips, she lifted up her skirt to reveal her hot pink, polka-dot slip, checking to make sure it could not be seen from the outside. She picked up her pocketbook and her pink cane that looked like a giant knitting needle, and put the black bottom back on, so that it now resembled and was able to be used as a cane. Before she left the house, she put yogurt, vegetables and water in the dishes for the shysters should they come home before her, and walked out to her garage to get in her car.

Granny parked in front of Nail's Hardware Store. She stopped to pat the Wrench Bench before opening the door and listening to the nail chimes alert Mr. Nail that she was in the store. Just as Granny walked in the door and the chimes started singing, she heard a loud crash, a big thump, a low moan and then silence.

Granny ran to the back of the store, past the hammers and the wrenches. She grabbed a hammer and held on to her pink cane in case she encountered questionable activity when she arrived in Mr. Nail's backroom. The first thing Granny saw when she entered the back room was collapsed storage shelves, and bags of fertilizer piled on top of the broken shelves. Granny could hear a groan coming from under the mountain of fertilizer. Then the groan stopped and there was dead silence.

Granny moved forward slowly and carefully, not wanting to disturb the precarious pile but just enough so that she could peek around the mound to see if she could find where the silenced groan had been.

"Mr. Nail? Mr. Nail? Is that you? Can you hear me? Are you ok?" Granny asked as she lifted her cell phone to call 911. Just as she did that, she saw a hand sticking out from underneath the mountain of fertilizer bags.

"Dad, what happened? What happened?" Neil Nail rushed into the room and over to the hand that was peeking out of the mountain. Granny tried to stop Neil by trying to block him with her cane but because she was on the phone, it was to no avail. Neil was sobbing on the floor grasping the hand.

"We need an ambulance and the police at Nail's Hardware," Granny yelled into the phone. "Mr. Nail had a mountain of fertilizer fall on top of him."

Granny hung up the phone and crawled over some of the bags to get to Neil. "Neil, honey; help is coming. Can you feel a pulse?" Granny reached over and moved Neil's hand to see if she could feel a heart beating in what she thought must be a lifeless body underneath the mountain. She really wanted to scream but she had to be strong for Neil. Just as Granny was going to tell Neil there was no hope, the ambulance and the fire department arrived along with the Big Guy. Franklin wasn't far behind.

Granny tapped Neal with her cane. "Neil, we have to move so they can help your father." Granny wished she now had her umbrella with the crook in it so she could just hook Neil's arm and drag him away. "Neil," Granny said in her sternest tone, "Move it, move it, move it."

Neil gave Granny a dazed look but got up and followed Granny to the side of the storage room so the fire department could get the collapsed shelves and bags of fertilizer off of Mr. Nail. The Big Guy walked over to both of them.

"Can you tell me what happened, Granny? Again, you seem to be in the middle of disaster."

Granny gave him her harshest look, poked him with the top edge of her cane and advanced on him, finally looking him straight in the eye. "What are you implying? I came here to pay Neil. I heard the ruckus in the back room, ran back and saw the collapsed shelves and fertilizer and then I called you."

"I'm sorry, Granny, I didn't mean anything by it. It seems like we have bodies everywhere lately. Neil, what can you tell me? Were you here when this accident happened?"

Neal looked at him through glazed eyes. "No, I came in right after it happened. Granny was in the back room and there was my father underneath all the bags of fertilizer. It's my fault; it's all my fault. I stacked those bags of fertilizer. I was in a hurry because I had work to do at my new house. I bought Mrs. Periwinkle's. If I had just taken more time." Neil started sobbing, burying his head in his hands.

Franklin, who had been watching the fire and ambulance crews, came over to the small group. "I'm sorry, Neil; your father is gone. Granny, can you take Neil out front so we can clear up this mess and the Big Guy can investigate the cause of this accident."

"I'm kind of wobbly. Neil, can you help me get out front?" Granny said in the weakest voice she could muster.

Neil, immediately hearing the tone in Granny's voice, stopped sobbing and helped Granny out front. "Are you ok, Granny? I'm sorry; this must be a shock for you too. You found him."

"I do feel a little faint. Maybe you could get me some coffee." Mr. Nail always had a little refreshment around if Granny needed it. Usually she had coffee that he kept in a thermos after purchasing it at Ella's Enchanted Forest in the morning. Granny thought that perhaps finding her coffee would help Neil get himself together a little bit before he had to deal with the details of his father's death.

Neil went behind the counter to grab his dad's thermos but it wasn't there. "Sorry, Granny, all Dad has here is lavender tea. In fact, he has boxes of it in the back room. Said a salesman talked him into it one day, saying it was the finest tea leaves around and a box of lavender tea would be perfect to give to his customers as a thank you gift."

At the words, *lavender tea*, Granny stood up. "Lavender tea? Think I'll pass on that," Granny answered, thinking of Sally and Mrs. Periwinkle. "Neil, why don't you go home and take a rest? You will have a lot to deal with. I'll have the Big Guy come over and talk to you later and I am sure Graves Mortuary will be calling."

Neil looked toward the back room. "I'm not sure I should leave."

"It's ok, Neil, things are in good hands with me. There is nothing more you can do here." Neil turned around as if to say something, shook his head, wiped a tear out of his eye and walked out the door muttering that it was all his fault.

Granny started heading toward the back room when the Big Guy stopped her. "Time for you to leave, Granny. Nothing suspicious here anyway. The shelves were old and collapsed, and Mr. Nail just happened to be in the wrong place at the wrong time." As the Big Guy finished his sentence, he started ushering Granny toward the door.

"Granny, didn't you say you had an appointment with the Mayor at 2:00?. It's just after 12:00; maybe you should go over to Rack's and get a bite to eat," said the Big Guy. "You look a little peaked and you may want to whip up some strength for the meeting with the Mayor."

"What did you do now?" Franklin asked as he came out into the front of the store. Then he winked at Granny.

"You're all trying to get rid of me. Something's up." Granny pounded the end of her fake cane on the floor.

"We'll let you know." Franklin took Granny's arm, ushered her out the door and locked it.

Granny turned and looked at the street. There was no one mulling around. It was pretty quiet, not usual for Fuchsia when there had been a suspicious death. Granny trekked down the street, deep in thought, shuffling her feet through the leaves that had fallen on the ground. As she was shuffling, she felt her toe hit something solid. She leaned down and picked up a large key that appeared to be very old. The handle had some rust on it but the part that fit into a lock, the old type of lock, was shiny as if someone had cleaned it recently. It almost resembled a skeleton key but unlike a skeleton key it had a little different configuration. There was a tag attached to it and the tag was labeled with a triple X.

Granny turned the key over in her hand, noted the time on her cell phone and threw the key in her purse to look at it closer when she got home.

Rack's restaurant was always busy at noon. As Granny headed back to her normal booth, she happened to turn her head to the right. When she did that her head stayed turned to the right and her body quickly followed her head. "Change of destination," she said to herself.

Sitting right across from the bar was Thor and that floozy who now lived across the street from her house. Granny plopped down in the booth right next to Thor.

"Am I interrupting anything?" Granny asked innocently.

"I was just asking Elena to marry me, but other than that...." Thor winked at Elena. Elena hid her smile.

"What! You just met! She's too old for you and look at the way she's dressed." Granny glared at Thor.

Thor started laughing. "Gotcha!"

Granny gave him the evil eye. Pretending to signal for the waitress, Granny knocked Elena's glass of water over and onto Elena's lap. Elena jumped up but not before the entire glass of water had spilled in her lap.

"I am soooo sorry," Granny said as she hung her head trying to hide her smile. "Can I help you clean it up?" Granny stood up as if to help. Elena moved away from the booth.

"I...guess I had better go home and change. It's ok, Granny. I know you didn't mean any harm." Elena leaned over the table and gave Thor a kiss on the cheek. "See you later," she said in a flirtatious voice and walked down the aisle and out of the restaurant.

Thor laid his head on the table and with great reserve on his part, pounded the table gently with both arms. "What was that? Maybe my sisters are right."

Granny quickly hailed down her waitress trying to get Thor's mind off of his sisters. "My usual," she said to the waitress, "and make it fast, I have a meeting with the Mayor."

"What's that all about?" Thor asked suspiciously.

"I don't know, maybe he's going to fire me."

"Fire you from what?"

"There's something I haven't told you."

"Surprise, surprise," moaned Thor. "What kind of trouble have you gotten yourself into now? Don't you think kidnappers and almost getting yourself aced so that we actually would have to put that silly rhyme you made up on your tombstone is enough?"

Granny squared her shoulders, took a drink of her coffee thinking that Rack's coffee wasn't half as good as the Boneyard Coffee & Tea Specialty coffee being served at Ella's, closed her eyes and started to speak.

"Well, you see, I am employed by the merchants of Fuchsia as their undercover sleuth. I catch shoplifters and stop them, and then the Big Guy swoops in and arrests them. It was no accident that I was involved with the investigation of the kidnappings and thievery that was happening."

Thor turned and looked at her with raised eyebrows. "I now understand why my sisters might be concerned. Maybe living alone with those daffy animals—yes, I know all about them. Now you are making things up."

"Just in time," Granny remarked to the waitress as she brought Granny's food. Granny looked down at her plate and it was a healthy salad. Everyone in Rack's knew that when Granny was with her kids, she ate healthy instead of her usual favorite foods.

Thor and Granny ate the rest of the meal in silence.

Granny decided to forgo her usual dessert as it was almost 2:00 and she didn't want to be late for her meeting with the mayor. Granny kissed Thor on the cheek as she got up. "See you later."

Thor stood up and threw money for the check on the table. "Since you ruined my date, I might as well tag along with you and see what the mayor wants."

Granny gave Thor a look of alarm. "Don't you have something better to do with your time? Like mow your lawn?"

"Nope, I'm between jobs, remember? I can mow my lawn anytime. I think this will be much more interesting." He took Granny's arm and led her out of Racks.

Since Ella's Enchanted Forest was not too far down the street from Rack's, they walked. They had to go past Nail's Hardware. It was closed up tight with no lights on and a big closed sign on the door. Granny let out a sigh.

"You're going to miss Mr. Nail, aren't you?" Thor asked.

"Yes, but I feel really bad for his son Neil. He has no one else. Maybe I should adopt him into our family."

There was a big crowd milling around Ella's Enchanted Forest.

"What's this all about?" mused Granny. "I must have been mistaken. Maybe I don't have a meeting with the mayor. Maybe I dreamed it." Granny looked confused.

When Delight saw Granny enter her store, she and Ella ran to meet her. "Granny, we have a place for you right here in the Forest Room. We have it all set up with a latte with whipped cream on the top and a plate of your favorite donuts."

"Delight, what's going on? I thought I was supposed to meet the mayor."

"He's here, Granny. He has an announcement to make and he requested that you sit at the table with him."

"On second thought, Delight, I think I forgot that I left my bacon burning on the stove this morning and I have to go home before my house burns down." Granny turned to go back through the crowd to exit the building. Just as she did that, Thor and Franklin each took an arm and led her to the mayor's table.

"Oh, no, you don't, Hermiony," Franklin instructed. "You will sit here until the mayor has his meeting with you. You don't want to lose your job. You know, he's the boss." Franklin pulled out the chair for Granny. "I'll see you later. Thor and I will be over here. Got to get to know my future stepson." Franklin winked at Granny and was gone before Granny had time to protest.

Just as Granny started to get up to go after Franklin, the mayor sat down and the Fuchsia High School Band started marching into the building playing a song

Granny had never heard. Of course, that wasn't unusual, because to be in the Fuchsia High School Band you didn't have to be good, you only had to have the desire to play. According to the Fuchsia Band Director "There are no wrong notes."

Granny could have argued that at this point but she was so astounded at what was happening that she was speechless. As she turned around, she saw the shysters and Baskerville all sitting by Franklin. *How did they get here? Was that Angel petting Tank and Furball? What could the mayor possibly have to say to her in the middle of all this hoopla?*

Granny turned to the mayor, giving him the eagle eyed stare of an interrogator. "What was it you wanted to talk to me about? We can't talk here with all these people."

"Patience, Granny," Mayor Horatio Helicourt held up his hand, indicating Granny needed to be quiet.

At that moment, the band stopped playing and the Big Guy stepped to the microphone.

He held up both hands so everyone would quit talking but no one was paying any attention. Granny, frustrated with the whole scenario and wanting to get on with her talk with the mayor after this, whatever it was, stood up and yelled across the room over the noise of the crowd to Baskerville. "Howl, Baskerville, howl!" Baskerville heard her and put his snout in the air and howled the loudest blood curdling howl that his big body could give. Silence ensued.

The Big Guy continued, "Thank you, Baskerville; thank you, Granny. The mayor graciously gave me a few moments before the ceremony begins to update you on the recent crimes in Fuchsia.

"Ceremony? What ceremony, Horatio?" asked Granny.

"All in good time, Granny; all in good time. Let's see what the Big Guy has to say."

"As you know," continued the Big Guy, "a few weeks ago, our good friend Sally Katilda was found dead in her yard. Then a few weeks later, Esmeralda Periwinkle was found dead in her home. The autopsies showed that they both died of strychnine poisoning, not spelled like my last name, by the way. Today we had the sad death of Mr. Nail. Our sympathy goes out to his surviving son Neil Nail. Neil couldn't be with us today as the grief was too much for him to bear. He also bought Mrs. Periwinkle's house—that and today's findings were too much for him and he felt he couldn't face the public of Fuchsia yet."

Granny looked around the crowd, trying to catch Franklin's eye, but he was fixated on watching Angel pet Furball and Tank. Granny turned to Horatio and whispered, "What happened after Mr. Nail's accident? I was there and the bags of fertilizer just fell on him. Didn't they?"

Horatio pretended he didn't hear Granny and nodded toward the Big Guy as if to tell Granny that she needed to listen.

"It is with great regret and sadness that I have to announce that Mr. Nail was the perpetrator in Sally and Esmeralda's death. Not only did he give them the lavender tea as a free gift which was laced with strychnine and the cause of their deaths, but he gave it as a free gift for buying fertilizer for their lawns that actually had a potent mixture to grow weeds fast and ruin the grass in their yards. Although Mr. Nail's death was an accident, we found enough evidence against Mr. Nail during our investigation of his death to conclude that he killed Sally and Esmeralda. We still do not know his motive for the deaths but we will continue to investigate. But for all intents and purposes, the case is closed."

"NO!" yelled Granny. "That is so wrong! Mr. Nail would never have done that!" Granny jumped up and pointed her cane toward the Big Guy. The shysters, hearing Granny's protest, started barking and meowing.

Mayor Horatio Helicourt at that moment, apparently decided this might be the time to tell Granny why she was here. He stood up, signaled to the band to play the *Bond 007* theme, grabbed Granny's arms and half lifted her to the microphone at the front of the the room. It was a strange site with Horatio lifting Granny and moving her along with her feet dangling and moving like she might be running. Since Horatio had her arms pinned down, Granny couldn't tap him with her cane.

Horatio set Granny down on her feet next to the microphone and immediately started speaking before Granny could protest. "My fair citizens of Fuchsia, today I want to announce some major changes that are going to take place in our community. You are all aware that a few weeks back, Hermiony, (the name Hermiony got him a hard glare from Granny) found some unknown underground streets beneath the main street of Fuchsia and older neighborhoods in the town when in her crabbiness she hit the baseboard on the side of a wall in AbStract and fell into the underground streets accidently."

At the word *crabbiness*, Granny started to exit through the crowd, but Franklin stopped her exit and escorted her back to the mayor.

"Because of this accidental find of the underground streets, Granny also uncovered a crime and kidnapping ring in our very own city that was using the underground streets for ill-gotten gains. The City Council and I have decided to open the underground streets and maintain them for your shopping pleasure and for making running your errands easier in bad winter weather. We have some very clever ideas that we hope to institute soon."

Granny was then joined by Delight and Ella as the mayor continued speaking. "One of the first changes we are making which was unanimously agreed upon by this council is using this room, which was once the Forest Room for Ella's, for a mortuary. Graves Mortuary will take over Ella's Enchanted Forest."

The crowd erupted in protest as they loved Ella's. Delight and Ella started throwing donuts out into the crowd to silence them. It got the crowd's attention so the mayor was able to continue speaking. Granny was staring at him in complete disbelief, her mouth open but no words came out. Granny was speechless at the news, though Delight had hinted this might happen.

"Settle down, you will like what is to come. The reason we are moving Graves Mortuary to Ella's Forest Room is the fact that it was built to house a mortuary with a lift down into the streets below with a street underground to the mausoleum in the cemetery. The mausoleum will be expanded so that internment services can be held inside at the cemetery before the person is buried. You can all be warm and comfortable at such difficult times your life. Now I will turn the microphone over to Delight and she will explain the rest."

Delight stepped forward. Granny tried to leave again as she had no idea why she was up front and center. This time Ella and the mayor grabbed her to keep her from leaving.

"I am so delighted," Delight giggled. "Of course I'm delighted—I'm Delight," she giggled again, "by this turn of events. We are moving. The city of Fuchsia is going to build us a new shop where Graves Mortuary is now. It will be shaped like a teapot and a coffeepot hooked together and it will have a sunroom shaped like a donut. It is all I have ever dreamed about and now it is going to be a reality thanks to Granny and the City of Fuchsia."

At the mention of her name, Granny was about to protest that she didn't have anything to do with this teapot thing, when Delight continued her speech.

"Until then, we will set up our Coffee and Tea Shop in the Fire hall. They have generously offered us the space as long as the firemen get free coffee, tea and donuts while we are there. Our new place hopes to be up and running by New Year's Day. It will be the perfect start for the New Year." Delight giggled and motioned for the mayor to step forward to the microphone.

"None of this would be happening without Hermiony Vidalia Criony Fiddlestat. Because of her, we in Fuchsia can embrace life more comfortably in the winter. Because of Granny, our streets are safer and so in honor of what she has done for our community, I would like to present her with a key to the city of Fuchsia." He turned to present the key to Granny.

Delight nudged Granny forward. Granny turned to look at Delight, looked out at the crowd and saw Franklin wink at her and felt a large key in her hands. Granny looked up at the mayor. *Was she dreaming? She always dreamt about receiving the key to the city. Was this all a dream? Maybe she was hallucinating.* Granny looked down at her feet. *Maybe she should remove the rubber end of her cane and skewer herself to see if she was awake.*

Granny looked up to see the crowd standing on their feet; she heard applause; she looked at the key in her hand. She looked up one more time at the mayor and then she fainted dead away.

CHAPTER SIXTEEN

Granny opened one eye and found herself staring into a bright light. She then opened the other eye and still found herself seeing the light. "Am I dead? I have to go back. I have a crime to solve. I have to go back."

"Mom, mom, you're not dead," Thor assured his mother.

"I'm not? Then where am I? All I can see is the light calling me."

"Turn your head to the side. You're looking into the examining light that the doctor is shining into your eyes. You're in the emergency room. You fainted."

Granny quickly sat up, pushing the doctor's arm aside as she looked around the room. Thor, Franklin, the Big Guy, Delight, Ella, and the mayor were all in the room staring at her.

"What are you all staring at? You never saw a woman faint from surprise before? Or was it a dream? Did you really give me the key to the city?" Granny asked as she turned to the mayor.

"I did," Horatio answered, "And then you went down like an apple dropping from a tree."

"Well, I'm apparently fine now. So you can all quit gawking and go on with your business." Granny thought for a minute realizing that they were worried about her. "I'm sorry I worried you. I know you were all concerned, and thank you for the honor of the key to the city. Go on now. I am going home."

"Granny," said the doctor holding the examining light, "as I told your son and your friends and the Big

Guy, I am concerned about this faint. I ran some blood tests and I don't have the results yet. I would like you to stay."

"And you are? I've never met you before, Doctor. Who are you and why should I trust you?"

"Pardon me for not introducing myself, but you were a little distant when they brought you in," the doctor said with a twinkle in his eye. "I'm Dr. Dreamboat, the new doctor at Fuchsia General Hospital."

"Why, you're just a youngster. When did they start letting kids be doctors?"

"When they started letting old ladies catch crooks," Dr. Dreamboat quipped right back at Granny.

Granny looked the doctor up and down while the others who had been in the room filed out laughing, leaving Thor and Franklin hiding their chuckles. Perhaps Granny had met her match.

"Got a little spunk in ya Doc. How 'bout we make a deal? I won't try and hook you up with any of Fuchsia's single women if you let me go home with Thor and Franklin to wait for my blood tests. I got things to do and I feel perfectly fine—well, as fine as someone my age can feel."

Dr. Dreamboat looked at Thor and Franklin. "Do you think you two can handle her?"

"Just watch us, Doc," Thor answered as he moved forward. Franklin moved forward with him. Thor picked up Granny's pocketbook and cane while Franklin picked up Granny.

"We'll talk to you later, Doc." Franklin told the doctor as he walked out of the room with Granny in his arms.

Granny knew this was the time to not protest if she wanted to get out of there, but there was going to be payback later for this armed hijacking.

Once back at Granny's house, Franklin made sure Granny was comfortable on the sofa while Thor decided to whip up some food.

"He tried to burn my house down last time, Franklin," Granny protested. "Don't let him cook. I'm not hungry. I just want my donuts and candy."

"Relax, Mom; I am doing stir fry with tofu. You'll like it."

"It's time for you to go—both of you. I need my beauty rest." Just at that moment, the pet door flopped open and Fish, Little White Poodle, Furball and Tank bounded into the room, all running to Granny. Furball hopped on her head, Little White Poodle and Fish hopped in her lap and Tank sat on her feet. "See, I'm perfectly fine here. The shysters will take care of me," Granny cajoled.

All of a sudden, the window door popped open and Baskerville bounded in followed by a small goat. Baskerville ran over to Granny and started howling and the little goat that was following Baskerville started bleating.

"What! What!" Granny shouted. "What is that! Who does that thing belong to? Baskerville, that is a goat and it is not mine. Take it back!!!"

Thor quickly came over and grabbed the goat.

Franklin soothed Granny. "Calm down, Granny. We will take care of it. Until we know whose it is, we don't want you upset."

"It belongs to that floozy across the street. Not only do I have to live across the street from a fake daughter of Sally's, but now she's trying to torment me with this goat!"

"She's a nice lady, Mom. You need to get to know her," Thor advised, still holding on to the goat.

Granny stood up, toppling the pets from her lap. She looked Thor straight in the eye. "She is a fake, I tell you. Sally did not have a daughter. Read my lips. Stay away from her," Granny warned Thor.

Thor looked at Franklin. "I'll take the goat back and let you handle this."

That did it. "I do not need handling!" screamed Granny. "I am fine." She picked up her pocketbook and her cane and stomped off to her bedroom, slamming the door, but not before warning Thor one more time, "Evil, I say! Evil!"

Granny opened her closet door and pulled out her purple workout clothes. They were more comfortable than the black dress and respectable shoes she was wearing. She thought she might try going to the basement to work out but that probably wouldn't be allowed by the gestapo in her living room. Granny plopped down on her bed to think about the day's happenings. Maybe she should call Neil Nail and see how he was doing. Not only was his dad dead, but they were accusing his father Mr. Nail of killing Sally and Esmeralda. Granny was trying to remember where she had left her cell phone when she heard a knock on her door.

"Granny, the Big Guy is here. He has the results of your blood test and he needs to talk to you," Franklin hollered through the door.

Granny opened the door and patted Franklin on the cheek. Franklin looked confused by that display of affection which was just what Granny wanted. She had decided she needed to change her tactics so she could go on with her investigation into Sally's and Esmeralda's deaths.

"See, nothing to worry about," Granny announced to the Big Guy when Granny arrived in the living room.

The Big Guy looked a little uncomfortable as he made eye contact with Franklin who had followed Granny back into the room.

"Granny, I think you need to give up your work for the merchants of Fuchsia. I will take your resignation now."

"What! I have no intention of resigning. Have you lost your marbles?"

"It's for your safety."

"I'm safe. Who would want to harm an old woman?"

Again, the Big Guy made eye contact with Franklin. Franklin came forward and stopped in front of Granny. "Granny," continued the Big Guy, "your blood tests show you were poisoned. That's why you collapsed."

"Poisoned? That can't be possible," stated Granny. "Who would want to poison me and why? I haven't got anyone arrested recently except Tricky Travis Trawler and Tricky Travis isn't a murderer."

"We didn't say they wanted to murder you Granny." the Big Guy interjected. "The poison in your system wasn't enough to kill you; it was just enough to knock you out for a while. We think it was a warning."

"A warning for what?"

"We don't know," Franklin said. We don't want to take any chances though."

"We also need to figure out how it got in your system. It was fast acting so it had to be something you had at Ella's Enchanted Forest," the Big Guy stated.

"Are you saying Delight poisoned my coffee or the mayor? Because he was the only one that was at my table."

"No," the Big Guy explained, "We have had everything you ate there tested. It had to be something else. Did you have anything else right before you got taken to the front of the room?"

Granny sat down on the couch to think. "I had a mint—a mint from the tin in my pocketbook." Granny got up and sprinted to her room to grab her pocketbook, digging in it as she came back out. "Here, here is the tin. I took a mint out right before I was taken to the front."

"Do you remember where you got these mints?" the Big Guy asked.

"No, I just found them in my pocketbook. I figured I had bought them and forgotten that I bought them. You know my memory. I don't usually buy mints so when I saw the mints in my purse I decided that I must have purchased them at some time." Granny looked at them as if this was a perfectly good explanation as to why the mints were in her purse."

The Big Guy took the mints from Granny. "I'll take these down to the station and have them tested and also test the box for prints. Of course, right now my prints and your prints are accounted for. You stay out of trouble."

The Big Guy instructed Granny as he walked out the door. "The doctor said there should be no ill effects from the poison. It should be out of your system by now."

"Well, then you can go too, Franklin. I need to talk to Thor to make sure he doesn't tell his sisters about this or I won't need any protection; I'll be in the Wrinkle Farm faster then you can say Wrinkle Cream. Where is Thor? Shouldn't he be back from that hussy's house? I need to go and get him. No telling what she'll do to him." Granny started for the door.

"Hermiony, leave it alone. He's old enough to do what he wants and she is awfully pretty."

At the word *pretty*, Granny grabbed her pocketbook and headed for her bedroom. "It's late, it's been a long day. I need my beauty sleep. You can let yourself out, Franklin." As Granny got to the bedroom door, she remembered her new strategy. "Oh, and Franklin, thank you for your concern." Granny walked back into the living room and up to Franklin, who was now standing by the door. Because he was such a large man it took all she could do to stretch high enough, getting as high on her tiptoes as she could to reach his cheek with her lips, giving his cheek a quick brush of a light kiss. Before Franklin could say anything, Granny sprinted back into her bedroom and shut the door.

Once Granny heard the door close, and was sure Franklin had departed, she quietly walked back into the living room and grabbed her binoculars, training them on Sally's house. Again, she could see two silhouettes in the window. Just as she was about to put down her binoculars, she saw the heads of the two silhouettes meet face to face. Soon she saw the blinds being drawn and the lights go out in Sally's house. Granny put down the binoculars and slowly made her way to bed, a thoughtful frown on her face.

Granny was in the middle of a dream or rather a nightmare. In it, Thor was kidding Elena, the floozy across the street. Granny was about to raise her giant knitting needle with the rubber tip missing from its body and save Thor from the clutches of the dangerous woman, when the phone ringing brought her out of the dream. "What?"

"Have you seen Baskerville?" Franklin's voice through the phone showed concern.

"Not since last night. He is probably out with the shysters. They should be at your house shortly after doing their rounds."

"Itsy and Bitsy, Fish and Little White Poodle are here but there is no Baskerville. He's always with them now."

Granny sat up in bed abruptly. "I'll take care of this. That hussy stole my son and now she's stolen my dog." Granny slammed the phone down, jumped into her flip flops, forgetting that it was almost winter, threw on her purple workout clothes that she had worn yesterday and dashed out of her house. She forgot to look both ways before crossing the street and was reminded that perhaps she should have when she heard the screech of tires right next to her ear. Mavis and George jumped out of their car that had almost hit Granny.

"Granny, what are you doing? We could have killed you—smash, splat, right on the ground, like a pancake!" Mavis declared.

"We went out for early morning pancakes; we didn't think we'd almost make a human one on our way home," George scolded.

"No time right now," Granny answered. "Your neighbor has kidnapped Baskerville and Thor." Granny continued on her way across the street, reaching the door of Sally's house—it was still Sally's house if Granny had anything to say about it. Granny started pounding hard and loud. George and Mavis followed Granny. They had seen Granny in this mode of operation before and it never ended well.

The door opened. "Why, Granny, what can I do for you? I am so sorry about last night. Thor explained about your accident; Didn't he say it was an accident? I can't remember. Anyway, I am so sorry about Gottlieb bothering you. Would you like some coffee? We should get to know one another since perhaps I might be your daughter-in-law someday." Elena said sweetly.

George and Mavis got to Granny just as it looked as if she was going to attack Elena. They grabbed her arms and lifted her away from the door.

"Unhand me. I was just going to give her a bear hug. You know the kind where the bear squeezes the person to death? Is Thor here? And where did you hide Baskerville?"

"Thor is not here, Granny. He is probably home in bed. I haven't seen that huge hound of yours. What makes you think he's here? And I am so sorry about yelling at you before about your critters. Thor explained and if Thor can love those little hole diggers, so can I," Elena apologized in a meek tone.

"We have to go now," George explained to Elena as Mavis grabbed Granny's arm and started leading her back across the street.

Granny yelled back to George. "Ask her where her goat is. GetLeave or Gottlieb or whatever!"

"Perhaps we should call Franklin," Mavis suggested. "Or Thor. It seems you aren't over last night yet."

Granny was about to protest Mavis' suggestion, when Franklin drove up in his '57 black Corvette convertible. "What's going on?" Franklin asked Mavis as George came across the street and joined the group.

"Granny had a little run in with our nice, pretty little new neighbor Elena," George explained.

Both Mavis and Granny looked at George and said at the same time, "Nice? Pretty?"

Mavis walked over and grabbed George's arm. "Perhaps we should go home and work on a new reality show. It's called 'Pretty Little Neighbor Moves out of Town'."

Granny and Franklin watched George and Mavis walk home before continuing on into Granny's house. Granny was about to explain to Franklin what the problem was when they were greeted in Granny's living room by Baskerville and Elena's goat Gottlieb.

"Baskerville, why are you with that goat?" Granny asked, about ready to grab the goat when Baskerville jumped in front of Gottlieb to stop Granny. Every time Granny moved one way to get the goat, Baskerville moved right along with her to block her. Granny looked at Franklin. "It's your turn. Gottlieb needs to go home."

Franklin moved to grab Gottlieb when Baskerville howled, jumped up and knocked Franklin off kilter, not knocking him down but disturbing his balance enough so that Baskerville and Gottlieb could run out the window door that had popped open when Baskerville howled.

Franklin and Granny ran and threw the front door open to catch them but all they caught was a glimpse of them running down the street.

"What do we do now?" Franklin asked Granny. At that moment Franklin's cell phone rang. Granny listened in as he answered the call.

"What? Keep them there. I'll be right there. I've got to go, Granny. My daughter needs me. I will get Baskerville and that mangy goat. You stay put and get some rest." Franklin hustled down the steps, got into his car and disappeared down the street.

Granny turned to go back into her house when she heard another car start up. It was the hussy backing out of her garage at the back of her yard. Granny watched as she too drove down the street in the same direction Franklin's car had gone. Granny turned to see if there was life at Thor's house. How did he miss all this ruckus? Granny checked Mavis and George's house and she could see them having an animated conversation in their living room. Granny turned to look at Sally's house. She turned, stepped into her house long enough to find her cell phone and her knitting needle cane, stepped out and closed the door. Nonchalantly she started strolling toward Sally's house, carefully checking to make sure no one was looking.

CHAPTER SEVENTEEN

Granny made sure she looked in both directions before crossing the street since she almost ended up as flat as a pancake the last time she decided to visit Sally's house. She still wanted to make sure that the coast was clear.

She decided to see if possibly the hussy had left the door open in her haste to leave. Granny walked up to the door, looked around, checking to see that no one was watching and turned the knob. The knob turned and Granny heard the latch of the door open. She gently pushed slowly on the door to open it a crack and peered in through the crack to make sure no one was there. Then she gave a little "ha hoo" to see if anyone answered. They didn't. Granny quickly moved her body all the way inside the house and shut the door.

Granny looked around the kitchen. It was the same as when Sally lived there. She moved further into the house. Everything was the same. When she checked the room that had been Sally's bedroom everything was the same there too including Sally's stuff still in the closets and drawers. *Why was everything the same?*

Granny continued on to what had been the guest bedroom. It looked like a whirlwind had hit this room. There were clothes strewn all over. Makeup littered the nightstand and the bed was still unmade.

Granny wondered why, if Elena had moved into the house and had been here at least for a few weeks, she had she not changed things if she was planning to stay.

Granny moved on to the basement. It looked like it had been in the remodel phase. Tools were set up but it looked like the construction had not gone very far. *Was Sally remodeling her basement?* Part of the wall had started to be cut out but the cut stopped halfway down from the ceiling. But hadn't the basement been empty when Granny had peered through the basement windows on her earlier snoop trip?

Granny decided she would ponder the thought of what was happening in this basement, but she knew she was running out of time before the hussy would come back and she still wanted to check out the garage. Granny headed back upstairs to the door off the kitchen. She opened it a crack and peered out to make sure no one was watching. The coast was clear so she stepped outside shutting the door behind her making sure the door was all the way shut. She started to walk to the back yard, checking to see that Mavis and George were not watching, but then on second thought she turned back and wiped off the handle of the door with her top to make sure she didn't leave any fingerprints.

As she stood in the backyard surveying the now dying weeds because of the fall weather, Granny decided to check out the garage. She walked to the back of the yard along the driveway and touched the handle on the door on the side of the garage. It moved and so she twisted it a little more and opened the door. Checking to make sure no one was watching, she moved all the way inside.

There didn't seem much to see inside. The garage was empty except for a pen where Gottlieb must be kept. His bowls were filled with food and water and there was a place for him to sleep. Since Granny didn't know much about goats, she didn't know if this was a good way to keep a goat or not. Granny did notice a heater that would keep the garage warm in the cold weather so Gottlieb would have warmth. Granny made a note in her mind, to check out the care of goats. Maybe she could report the floozy/hussy to the Humane Society so she didn't have to deal with Mr. Bleaty.

As Granny was considering the thought of the Humane Society, she heard a car drive up the driveway and the garage door start to lift. She quickly ran to the side door, ran out and decided to hide on the other side of the garage. As she was running past what looked to be an old water pump, Granny tripped over something large hidden in the weeds and fell flat on her face. She turned her head to the right and saw a small, round stone structure sticking out of the ground. Her eyes went wide realizing that had she fallen mere inches to her right, that stone might have actually closed her eyes forever. She was ready to lift herself off of the ground when she heard the side door of the garage open. Granny stayed still, hidden by the tall dying weeds.

Granny peered through the weeds and listened for the opening and closing of the house door. When she was sure the coast was clear, she sat up first checking to make sure no one was watching.

Granny examined the round stone structure that poked out of the ground. It appeared to be an old cistern. Sally's house had been built on land that had been cleared when the original home on the property had burned many years ago. Apparently the old property still had the old cistern that had held rainwater. Granny hadn't noticed it before because she had never been this far back in Sally's yard or on this side of the garage. Not too far from the cistern was an old pump from an old well. Apparently it had never been sealed but that was not so surprising since Fuchsia pretty much let homeowners do what they wanted with their property, following the old motto *Your Home Is Your Castle*.

Lifting herself off the ground cautiously, Granny decided it was time to wind her way home. Gottlieb was not in the garage but where was Baskerville?. Since she was on the side of Sally's that led into the trees because no more houses had been built on that edition, Granny decided the trees were her best bet for getting back into her yard unseen. Her yard also sat next to the trees but her yard was big and sat empty across from Sally's house. Granny, after all of these years, was still trying to decide what to do with that piece of empty property.

As she walked back farther into the trees so it looked like she would have been taking a fall stroll in nature, she came out on her side and decided to sit down on an old stump to rest. Sitting there among the trees reminded Granny of the farm where she had grown up that was still outside of Fuchsia. She hadn't been back there for many years. It must now look like an abandoned farm. Her kids didn't know that she still owned that piece of property. Her parents had left it to her. She didn't think about it often. Her past was in the past. She didn't go there often in her mind.

Granny heard a rustle in the grass a few yards away. It was a skunk. Granny decided that it was time to head home. "Mr. Skunk, I know you stunk, but if you try and spray me," Granny lifted a big rock ready to heave, "I'm going to give you a big thunk." The skunk looked at Granny; Granny looked at the skunk. It was a stare down and then they both retreated, slowly walking backwards. never taking their eyes off of each other.

As Granny came out of the woods, she saw Franklin's car parked in front of her house. As she got close to the door, she heard the sound of laughter. Granny opened the door to her house and found the source of the laughter that she had heard while she was coming up the steps of the porch. It was Angel, the little girl who lived in Mrs. Shrill's house. She was playing ball with Tank and Little White Poodle while Baskerville was sitting next to her and Fish and Furball were sitting on the back of the couch trying to bat the ball as it sailed past them in the air on its way to its destination on the floor.

Franklin and Angel's mother Heather were talking by the window while keeping an eye on the goings on in the living room. They both turned when Granny walked into the room. Angel, seeing Granny, ran up to her and said, "Hi, Granny. I am playing with Itsy and Bitsy and Fish and Little White Poodle. Baskerville is helping me."

Granny looked at Franklin with a questioning look in her eye before bending down to Angel's level to talk to her. "I see that. I didn't know you knew where I lived. And how do you know Tank and Furball—uh Itsy and Bitsy to you?"

"'Cause my Grandpa came and picked up Baskerville from my house. That's how I know where you live. Grandpa said we could come along and bring Baskerville home and Itsy and Bitsy are my Grandpa's pets," Angel rattled on. "My Grandpa said that it was time we meet you since you are going to be my Grandma so I can call you Granny now. When I told you my other Granny is far away, I meant heaven and now I am going to have a real live Granny again." Angel stopped the rambling and threw her arms around Granny and gave her a big hug."

Granny put her arms around Angel and turned her around while she was doing it so she could look Franklin straight in the eyes. Franklin answered that questioning and piercing look by winking at Granny.

Granny stood up while still holding on to Angel. "Why don't you go and continue playing with the shysters in the back yard while I talk to your Grandpa. I think you should be safe back there. Baskerville will protect you. If it's ok with your mom, that is."

Heather nodded her head and all the furry creatures followed Angel out the door, winding their way to the back of the house on the path along the side the house.

As Granny turned and eyed Franklin, Franklin stepped forward. "Granny, I would like you to meet my daughter Heather. She just moved here recently."

Heather put out her hand to shake Granny's. "Nice to meet you again Granny. I wanted to tell you sooner who I was but my dad thought it would be better, considering everything you have been through, to wait until the time was right. Baskerville seemed to provide that time."

"Um, nice to meet you, Heather."

"I better check on Angel. I'll leave you two to talk." Heather winked at her dad as she walked out the door to find Angel.

"You didn't think to tell me this, Franklin Jester Gatsby, and would you mind telling me why that sweet child thinks I'm going to be her Grandma?" Granny picked up her cane and stomped it back down on the floor. Then she went over to her umbrella that was sitting in the corner, picked it up and pointed it at Franklin. "I'm not hearing you answer fast enough."

"Now, Hermiony, we're engaged. Don't you think it's time we told my kids? Your children know," Franklin said with a twinkle in his eye.

"Don't give me that, Franklin Gatsby. You know we're not engaged. You know that was just to keep my kids from harassing me about moving. Thor, Thor, my son, lives right across the street. Do you know how difficult it is doing my investigative work with these murders with Thor living right across the street and now, and now...." Granny started poking him with her umbrella tip, "...your daughter thinks we are engaged and that sweet child will be very disappointed when she finds out that she isn't going to have a live Granny again, that it was all pretend. This is on you when it falls apart. Do you hear me, Franklin Jester Gatsby? Do you hear me?" Granny stomped the umbrella on the floor and immediately retreated to her room in frustration. She didn't see the wide grin on Franklin's face as he left through the door because that was the exact reaction he was expecting and hoped for from Granny. She did drive him crazy but it was a good crazy and so much fun. He had never felt so alive.

Granny heard the door close. She reached in her pocket for her cell phone so she could see what time it was. When she didn't find it in her pocket, she walked into her living room and checked the sofa before continuing on into the kitchen. *Where had she put that cell phone?* Granny paused to look out the window and then she remembered. She had the cell phone in her pocket before she went to Sally's. She must have dropped it. It wouldn't be good for her to go over there right now and look for it. The hussy might get suspicious and know Granny was on to her. Granny looked at Mavis' house and she got an idea. She walked over and picked up her landline phone and dialed Mavis.

"Hello, would you like a reservation at Georgy Porgy Pudding and Pie Diner?"

"Mavis, what reality show are you into now? I need your help."

"Did you say you were wondering if we had scallops?"

"Mavis!" Granny said in her most threatening tone.

"All right, Granny, we were just having a little fun with a pretend reality show restaurant," Mavis giggled as she whispered something off to the side to George.

"I lost my cell phone next door at the hussy's house. She likes you and George. Can you go over and find it for me without making it suspicious."

"Why would it be there and where might we look?"

"Um, you don't need to know the reason I was there but you might want to look, um, in the kitchen, the bedrooms, the living room, the dining room, and, um, the basement."

"What! I don't want to know, Granny. How are we going to get into every room of her house?"

"Can't you tell her you want a tour and that you are scouting it for your new reality series *Disguise That House*? Oh, and one more thing, you might want to check the back yard and garage for my cell phone too. You have to find it before she does."

Granny heard a loud click. She hoped that meant they were on their way. She peeked out the window to see if there was any movement from Mavis' house. Sure enough, George and Mavis were on their way to Sally's house. Granny watched as they knocked on the door and handed the floozy something. Just as she seemed to be inviting them into the house, Mr. Bleaty (as Granny preferred to call him), bounded up the steps with something in his mouth. Granny could see large gestures and then George taking something out of Mr. Bleaty's mouth. They both turned as if to thank the floozy/hussy and then started to come over to Granny's. Granny quickly jumped out of the view of the window.

The doorbell chimed and Granny answered the door. Mavis handed Granny something that looked like a loaf of bread that was as heavy as a brick. "What is this?" Granny said to Mavis.

"That was our excuse to visit Elena. We baked bread in Georgy Porgy Pudding and Pies Kitchen and we are bringing our neighbors a loaf. Now let us in," Mavis begged.

Granny opened the door wider and George and Mavis came in. George reached in his pocket and handed Granny a crushed and half eaten cell phone.

"I take it this is yours," George told Granny. "I guess it is true about goats eating anything."

Granny held up the pieces of her cell phone and looked at it in dismay. "You didn't say this belonged to me, did you?"

"No," Mavis answered. "I told her it was mine and I must have dropped it when I chased Gottlieb back home after he had been in our yard. Although I hope she doesn't discover that Gottlieb never has been in our yard."

George took Mavis by the arm. "We have to go, Granny. Georgy Porgy has pig knuckles cooking in the kitchen and we have to get back to them. I hope you can get your phone fixed."

Granny shut the door after them and looked at the pieces of her cell phone. She glanced at the clock on the microwave and saw that it was just past noon. That surprised her since it seemed like she had put in an entire day's work.

Deciding that she needed her cell phone, Granny sprinted back to her bedroom, changed her clothes into her Granny skirt, red sparkly shoes, an old fashioned pin striped blouse and topped it off with a warm middle of the year navy coat. Navy wasn't usually her color but she figured she might need to be colorless when going to the phone store.

Granny decided to grab her umbrella instead of her knitting needle cane. It was getting cold and windy and it appeared like it might rain and sleet and, of course, there was always the chance she might get to hook a crook for excitement.

Allure, Minnesota, was the place with the nearest phone store. Granny hopped in one of her red Chevy

Corvettes to head out of town. She was going to miss having the top down now that the cold weather was setting in. That led her to wonder how the weeds in Sally's and Mrs. Periwinkle's yards could have grown so fast. Maybe now that it was fall and the weeds were dead, it would reveal something. Granny decided after the phone store that she would go back to Fuchsia and see if Neil Nail was going to reopen the hardware store. Somehow Granny had the feeling that there were more answers in the hardware store and that the police had closed the investigation too soon. As Granny stepped out of the car, a chill went up her back. She turned her head just in time to see someone snap her picture and drive away.

CHAPTER EIGHTEEN

Granny opened the door to the phone store. "Did you see that? That man was taking a picture of me. Call the police. I want to know who he was."

The young man behind the counter looked up as Granny entered. "Yeh, well, everyone's taking pictures now, ya know. No one's safe. Might end up on SciffScaff, the online video place. You never know who's takin' your picture. Were ya doin' something stupid?"

"Ah, no."

"Then why should you care? You're on camera all the time." The young man pointed to the ceiling. "Look up, see anything there?"

Granny peered at the ceiling. "Ah, no."

"Well it's there; right here and here and here." He pointed as he tapped on the ceiling in different places. "See that, cameras all over taking your picture." He walked to the front of the store. He pointed at the light pole right by Granny's car. "See that? Yup, it's there— a camera. I'd say a guy taking your picture is the least of your problems. You can see him. See that man who just passed you in the street? See his hat."

Granny peered out the window at the man walking down the street.

"It's taking a picture of you. All he has to do is meet you or follow you and it's done. You're recorded. You don't know what he's gonna do with that picture. Could be a Sciffscaff guy, and you wouldn't even know it." The young man stood next to Granny and put his arm around her shoulders, leaned in and whispered. "You never know who's watching you."

Granny jumped back wishing she hadn't forgotten her umbrella in the car or better yet, she wished she had her knitting needle. He would have seen that she got her point across.

"Enough!" Granny yelled. "I came for a phone and if you don't get me one soon, well, I don't want to be responsible for what happens." Granny grabbed his arm and led him over to the window. "You think I'm an old woman and you're gonna scare me, do ya? Well, let me let you in on a little secret. I'm not old; this is a disguise and I'm undercover. See that car out there? It is not just a car. See those headlights? They're not just headlights. They can take someone out in a second by a flip of a switch that's in my pocket. Granny indicated she was holding something in her pocket. "See that car door? If it opens by itself, well, I don't want to be responsible. Get me a phone!!! Lives are at stake." Granny took a tighter grip on his arm. "Do you understand?"

"Right, right. I'll be back in just a minute. I have just the right phone for you in the back room."

Granny meandered around the store looking at the fancy electronic tablets, at the phone cases, when she heard the door open and close. Two policeman entered the store and walked up to her.

"Is this the woman who threatened you?" one of the policemen said to the young man who was now standing in the door to the back room.

"Yes, yes it is. And she's not right. She said she's a secret agent. She told me her car could take me out."

Granny turned and looked at the young man with a piercing gaze. "And he told me everyone was taking pictures of me. He told me there are cameras in the ceilings and cameras in the light pole. He was clearly harassing an old woman. I was defending myself. I just came in to get a new cell phone!"

The officer looked at Granny and checked the ceiling and then pointed to the light pole. "Look, no cameras. Are you sure you didn't imagine him saying that to you?"

"Are you saying I'm daft? Ask him. Ask him."

"Officers, why would I tell an elderly lady that there were cameras everywhere watching her? Clearly, she has problems. In fact, she came in and told me there was a man taking pictures of her."

"Did you tell him that?" the other officer questioned Granny.

"I did, because there was. Listen, you need to call the Big Guy, Cornelius Stricknine of the Fuchsia Police Department. He will tell you, I work for them."

"Ma'am, you better come with us."

"Where?"

"The Allure Police Station, if this young man decides to press charges, then we have to arrest you."

"The Hoosegow? All I want is a cell phone."

The policeman looked at the young man. "Are you pressing charges?"

"Not if you can guarantee me that she will not stop here again."

"Get me a cell phone and you'll never have to see me again," Granny assured him.

The young man went over to the counter and picked out an Itphone for Granny, the latest one.

"What about my addresses that are stored in the raincloud? Can you put them on?"

The police officers looked like they were going to intervene again so Granny decided it was time to change her tactics. She started sniffling. "Please, I am so forgetful and I have no one." Granny started sniffling some more. "I don't know what happens to me. I get these lapses and then I behave out of character. My doctor is checking me Gottliebers' disease. If I did something strange while I was here I can't explain it."

The police officers looked at the young man who was giving Granny a piercing look. "Help her out. She clearly needs her phone and isn't capable of putting her numbers in. We'll take her for coffee and come back in a little while. We'll also try and get a hold of her family."

With that, they helped Granny out of the store and took her down the street to the corner coffee shop. Granny ordered her usual donuts and coffee. The police officers decided to do the same.

"What is the number of someone we can call for you, ma'am? What did you say your name was?"

"Granny."

"Granny what? Is that your real name?" the officer questioned.

"Who can we call?"

"I can't remember any of the numbers. I can't remember my name. Just Granny The numbers were all in my phone."

"How about a name to call?"

"The Big Guy, Cornelius Stricknine, Chief of Police, Fuchsia, Minnesota."

One of the officers got up to go out to his squad car to call the Big Guy. In the meantime, Granny took a look around peering out the window to see if she could catch a glimpse of anyone who looked familiar or like the man she had seen earlier taking her picture. The police officer returned to the table.

"We can let her go. The Big Guy vouched for her. Said she's a little bit eccentric but harmless and she is capable of taking care of herself and driving herself home. He said she was a bit cantankerous and had a penchant for finding trouble but he will take care of it."

The other officer stood up at the same time as Granny stood. "We'll walk you back to get your cell phone. We don't want any more incidents."

The three walked back down the street with one of the officers going inside to pick up Granny's cell phone, paying with her credit card and bringing the receipt outside for Granny to sign so there was no repeat of the earlier interaction between the young man and Granny.

Granny got in her car, waved to the officers and, characteristic of Granny, she stomped on the foot pedal and peeled her tires, leaving the officers shaking their heads as she headed out of Allure.

The closer Granny got to Fuchsia, the more she thought about Neil Nail and how he must be feeling now that his dad had died. Neil's mother was no longer in the picture so Neil would have to make all the funeral arrangements himself not to mention running the hardware store alone. Neil might dress a little young but he was old enough to be on his own and certainly capable of running the hardware business. Granny headed straight for Main Street when she got back to Fuchsia. As she pulled up outside of Nail's Hardware, she noticed Neil sitting out front on the Wrench Bench holding his head in his hands. He also didn't have a coat on and was shivering from the cold weather. Granny decided that he needed a friend.

"Neil, what' going on?" Granny asked as she sat down beside him on the Wrench Bench. "It's too cold to be sitting out here. Let's go inside the store."

"I can't. I can't. My dad died in there and it's all my fault." Neil broke down in tears."

Granny patted his hand. "Neil, it isn't your fault. It was a terrible accident."

"They think my dad killed those women. He didn't. I know he didn't. It's all my fault," Neal blurted out in spurts in between his sobs.

Granny had never seen Neil cry before and apparently her soft touch wasn't getting anywhere with him. Granny stood up.

"That's enough. Get yourself in that building and get warm before I have to go to my car and grab my umbrella. If I have to I'll hook it around your neck and drag you inside. You have a funeral to plan and a store to run. Your dad is watching you." Granny pointed to the sky. "He expects you to carry on."

Neil looked at Granny. "You don't understand. It's my fault."

"Well," Granny said, "Suppose you tell me, only inside. It's too cold out here for an old woman."

Neil got up off the bench and turned and unlocked the hardware store. He hesitated for a moment and then he turned to Granny. "Thank you, Granny, but I'll be alright now. I'm not supposed to let anyone into the store until the police say I can open it up again and the Big Guy said I am especially not supposed to let you in."

Granny was about to make a cynical retort but in view of Neil Nail's grief, she thought better of it. "Alrighty, I'll let ya off the hook this time. It's getting late anyway. It must be round about 4:00 p.m. I need to check on Delight in her new shop over at the fire station anyway."

Neil continued on into the store and Granny got in her car but not before she thoughtfully took a few minutes to think about what the reason could be that Neil thought the death of his father was his fault.

The Fuchsia Fire Station was hustling and bustling with all the firefighters sitting around drinking coffee and tea and eating Delight's donuts and other sweet confections, taking advantage of Ella's Enchanted Forest inhabiting their fire station. Granny saw that Delight had also made sure the candy that she made and sold, was front and center too. Those firefighters had a sweet tooth.

Fuchsia's Fire Department was full time. It wasn't because Fuchsia had a lot of fires but the mayor and Town Council felt that having a full time crew also was a way for the people of Fuchsia to feel safe. The firefighters also helped out with accidents, fire drills at Fuchsia School and used their equipment to build skating rinks in the winter. They also helped out at the pond, lake and waterpark in the summer as all the firefighters had their lifeguard certifications.

Granny spied Delight talking to Ella and a good looking young firefighter. "Woo Hoo, Delight!"

"Be with you in a minute, Granny." Delight seemed to be instructing Ella back to the kitchen while pointing somewhere at something that she thought the young firefighter should do. Then she made Granny's latte and put two lemon crème donuts drizzled with chocolate on a plate and brought them to Granny.

"What was that all about? I was about to come over and say 'hello' but you shooed them off."

"I'm not sure this was a good idea. All those good looking young firefighters seem to have caught Ella's eye. I am spending more time finding things for her to do away from the firemen and policemen.

"What about that young policeman I had escort Ella home after saving her in the underground streets?"

Delight was about to answer when a loud boom shook the fire hall almost knocking them over. Before they realized what had happened, bells and sirens went off in the fire hall announcing a fire. All the firemen dropped what they were doing and ran to the garage, getting their gear and taking off in the trucks.

Granny and Delight and the other customers watched them go. The sirens didn't go very far so everyone spilled out of Ella's Enchanted Forest Fire Hall cafe and ran down the streets in the direction of the trucks. From the next street down, black smoke was billowing into the air. As Granny and Delight walked further, they saw a few flames shooting out of the side of a building. To their horror, they realized Nail's Hardware was on fire.

CHAPTER NINETEEN

Granny, realizing what was happening, looked for the Big Guy. He was standing by the fire trucks along with Thor. *What was Thor doing here with the Big Guy?*

Granny grabbed the Big Guy's arm. "I was just here a few minutes ago. I left Neil walking into the hardware store." Granny said in alarm. "He might be still in there."

Thor walked over to his mother, and put an arm around her. "If he is mom, it's too late. Everything has collapsed."

The three of them stood side by side and watched as the Fuchsia Fire Fighters handled the fire.

As time passed, Thor turned to his mother, "It's getting late, you should go home. Do you want me to take you?"

"We're not going to know anything until later, Granny," the Big Guy explained. "The crew has to be able to get in there and then they will search for a cause and a body."

Granny shook her head. "You'll let me know. I must have been the last person who talked to Neil. He was blaming himself for his father's death and now he might be dead. I should have made him come with me." Granny walked away slowly still trying to process it all. When she got to her car, she decided to drive to Neil's house. After all, they could all be wrong; maybe he went home. They didn't even bother to check.

As Granny pulled up outside of Mrs. Periwinkle's house, she could see there were no lights on. Evening had descended during the fire since it got dark around 5:00 now. Maybe Neil had fallen asleep from exhaustion because of the last few days.

Granny got out of the car and walked to the front door. The door was locked. She walked around to the back of the house and tried the back door. It was open. Granny had brought her umbrella with her. She wished she would have brought her knitting needle cane instead of leaving it at home today. She could have used that cane to skewer the guy taking her picture outside the cell phone store so the policeman in Allure would have believed her. She could have also skewered that sniveling young man in the store into telling the truth. Granny stuck her umbrella inside the door for protection before she went in. She wasn't sure why she should need protection but you never knew.

"Woo hoo, Neil! Are you home?" There was no answer. Granny switched on the light by the door. *What is with all these people moving in and not changing anything?* Granny proceeded to check out the house but it was as if Esmeralda Periwinkle still lived in the house.

Granny decided to check out the basement. Granny shook her head in disbelief. This basement seemed to be under construction too and it had the same cut in the same place in the wall as in the basement at Sally's house. Granny was about to check out the wall a little bit closer when she heard the door closing and footsteps upstairs. Granny quickly flicked off the basement light that she had turned on when she got down to the bottom of the basement steps.

"Granny, Granny, where are you and what are you doing here?"

Granny shook her head in disbelief as she recognized the voice. "What are you doing here?"

The basement door opened and Granny could see the silhouette of the Big Guy at the top of the basement stairs.

"I'm the Chief of Police. I don't have to tell you that. However, if you come upstairs I might actually answer the question. Oh, and don't point that umbrella at me. Remember? I'm the good guy."

Granny made her way up the steps ready to defend her reason for being here.

"I take it you just happened to be here because you thought Neil might be here instead of in the hardware store?"

"Well, yes," Granny answered meekly.

"Me too," said the Big Guy. "We didn't find any bodies. So Neil wasn't in the hardware store. However, we did find where the fire originated and it was arson. You don't suppose Neil had anything to do with that, do you?"

"Well, he's not here although I didn't check the garage out back and, no I don't think he had anything to do with it. How could you?"

At that moment Granny's cell phone rang the Dragnet theme. She grabbed the phone out of her pocket and as she answered and was ready to put the phone to her ear, Franklin's picture popped up on her screen with a little picture of her in the corner. Granny almost dropped her phone. "Have you been spying on me, Franklin? What are you doing in my phone?" Granny flicked the 'off' switch on her phone. She looked at the Big Guy. "Arrest him. He's in my phone. He's watching me. How did that happen?" Granny now stared at the blank dark screen since the phone was turned off.

The Big Guy started laughing. "You must have eye to eye on your phone. You can see each other while you talk."

"I don't want him to see me. He can see where I am. He can see what I'm doing."

"Turn the phone back on, Granny. If you turn off eye to eye, then he won't see anything. Did you get a new phone? What happened to your old one?"

Granny had turned her new phone back on as she was trying to figure out how to answer that question since she didn't want the Big Guy to know she had been in Sally's yard. The phone rang. Dragnet theme again. Granny looked at it and answered this time, staring Franklin in the eye over her phone.

"Where are you?" Franklin bellowed. "Don't you remember someone tried to poison you? I haven't been able to reach you since this morning."

"I am with the Big Guy, so I'm safe. I just saw Thor. It is not your job to follow me. They all seem to be doing a good job of it." Granny countered. "Got to go, talk to you later." Granny hung up the phone and put it in her pocket.

"He does have a point. Someone did try to poison you. Go home, Granny." The Big Guy took Granny's arm and led her to the front door and unlocked it. I'll let you know when I find Neil."

It took Granny a few minutes for her eyes to adjust to the dark as she made her way down the steps. The Big Guy might be rid of her for now, but only because it was time to go home and grab some wine and some chocolates and put together what she had seen in Sally's house and Mrs. Periwinkle's house—two basements in the middle of remodeling. Both houses with dead owners and weeds in the yard—what could that possibly mean?

Granny parked her Corvette in her garage. On the way to her house, she glanced at Thor's home. It was dark. As she glanced toward Sally's home that was now inhabited by that goat-loving floozy, she saw two heads silhouetted behind the shades. Granny slipped out her cell phone. Maybe now was the time to try out that eye to eye feature. She dialed Thor's number.

Thor answered with a look of bewilderment on his face. "Mom, when did you get eye to eye?"

"That's a good name for it. Love my new cell phone feature. Now I can keep an eye on you. Who's that I see in the background? Isn't it a little late for you? Wanted to make sure you were ok. Mother's duty, you know. Remember, I'm keeping an eye on you. Look out the window."

Granny watched as Thor lifted the window shade at the hussy's house. She gave a smile and waved before walking into her house. Once in the house, she positioned herself by the window with her binoculars. Soon she saw Thor leaving and going to his house. Mission accomplished.

A loud bleat almost knocked Granny off of her feet in surprise. She turned around to see Mr. Bleaty cuddled by the couch with Baskerville. They had been sleeping. What was with the two of them? They seemed inseparable.

"All right, all right, I give it up for the night. Mr. Bleaty can stay tonight. You two better run downstairs by the fireplace in case the hussy comes calling, looking for him. Don't come up until morning I need my beauty sleep."

Both Baskerville and Mr. Bleaty got up and looked at her and then trotted down the steps to resume sleeping. Granny pulled out her bottle of wine from the ottoman, moved the pet bowl where she hid her chocolates, grabbed some sweets and sat down to ponder the events of the day.

As the wine and the chocolates disappeared, Granny took the time to get familiar with her new phone. Some of the weird things on her phone might come in handy in a pinch. Heading off to bed, she stopped to check the locks on her door and make sure that the shysters had eaten today since she hadn't been home at the same time the shysters were usually at her house. It was strange that Baskerville seemed to hang out with Mr. Bleaty instead of the shysters.

Granny decided she was too tired to change out of her clothes into one of her nighties. She would change and shower in the morning before figuring out a way to investigate Sally's and Esmeralda's houses and yards a little bit more closely. She was sure there was some connection. And where was Neil? Perhaps, by morning the Big Guy would have found him.

The dream started with Baskerville howling. Mr. Bleaty joined in on the chorus. Franklin was playing the drums and the strobe lights were flashing as the rhythm got louder. The band was joined by a chorus of sirens. They were in the fire hall and Delight was barbequing ribs, a new item added to her menu.

Granny lazily woke up. She could smell those ribs but now it smelled like Delight was burning them and Baskerville and Mr. Bleaty seemed to be howling and bleating right next to her bed. She opened her eyes and she could see lights flashing through the window, through the darkness. The pounding started on her door and she heard Thor and Franklin shouting as they pounded. All of a sudden, Granny felt Baskerville clamping his mouth on her arm and pulling her over the side of the bed. Mr. Bleaty started nudging her. Granny heard the window on the side by the front door being broken and soon Franklin and Thor were in her room.

Before Granny knew what was happening, she was hoisted into Franklin's arms and carried out her front door with Thor following behind, and Baskerville and Mr. Bleaty leading the charge. It all happened so fast that Granny wondered if she was still dreaming but when she saw the firemen putting out the flames that seemed to be leaping out of her garage roof she didn't have to pinch herself to know she was awake.

"My cars, my cars! Put me down! I have to get to my cars!"

Franklin set her down but still kept an arm around her shoulders to keep her from going anywhere. George and Mavis and even the hussy were standing across the street watching the flames eating her garage and her cars.

The fire chief, Chuck Ladder, came over to the group. "We need you to go across the street in case the cars explode."

"They won't explode," Granny informed him. "The gas tanks are empty. I drained the one for the fall and winter and I was cruising on fumes when I came back from Allure in the other. I forgot to get gas with all the excitement at Nail's. Believe me, it's safe."

The three men looked at one another. "We'll move," Franklin assured the fire chief. "She might have forgotten." Franklin hustled Granny across the street by Mavis, George and Elena.

As Granny watched the firemen, the Big Guy who had just arrived, came over to talk to the group. "Did any of you see anything?"

Granny turned to Franklin. "How did you get here so fast? You were here at the same time as the fire department."

"I saw the flames from Heather's house. I was watching Angel, and Heather just got home and so I was leaving to go home. When I got here, Thor was headed to your door."

"I looked out my front window and saw the flames and called the fire department and then I ran over to pound on your door," Thor informed his mother.

"Where are the shysters?" Granny asked. "I know they are not usually here this time of night but I want to make sure they are safe."

"They were at Heather's when I left. They stopped in to play with Angel tonight."

All Granny could do was stare at Franklin at that news. The more things changed, the more they didn't stay the same. Now even the shysters were changing their routines. They were all upsetting Granny's applecart. Granny looked at Sally's yard. Baskerville and Mr. Bleaty were lounging in the yard together, nuzzling each other. Granny shook her head in puzzlement.

"Again I ask, did any of you see anything?" the Big Guy repeated.

"What's there to see? My garage started on fire. Probably some faulty electrical wiring. I knew that electrician I had here last year was up to no good."

Chuck Ladder came over to join the group. "We've got the fire almost out. I'm sorry to say your cars are toast."

At the word *toast*, Granny sadly looked at her garage and then sat down on the ground.

Thor knelt down by her to make sure she was ok. Chuck Ladder continued speaking to Franklin and the Big Guy. "It was arson. Someone started the trash container next to the garage on fire. Any idea who might want to burn Granny's garage down? That's two arsons in one day."

"I'll put the police on high alert and you might want your firemen to keep on their toes too. I'm also going to put out an APB for Neil Nail too. This all has to be tied together. Granny, I'm going to put an unmarked car in front of your house for your safety. This is the second time now that someone has tried to harm you. It looks like a warning."

"Get real, an unmarked car? Have you looked at this street?" Granny remarked as she looked up at the Big Guy from her place on the ground. She held her arm out to Franklin to help her up since she didn't have her cane or her umbrella. "It's a dead end street. We only have so many houses. You don't think someone's going to notice an unmarked car?"

"Of course they will; that's the point. They'll stay away," the Big Guy remarked in exasperation.

Granny shook her head and started to walk across the street toward her house. The Big Guy, Franklin, Thor, George and Mavis followed Granny across the street. Elena watched them go and then walked, unnoticed into her back yard.

The fire from the garage was still smoldering as Granny stopped to survey the damage. Granny uncharacteristically wiped a tear out of her eye, hoping no one else would see. The group was silent as they looked at the charred remains of Granny's two red '57 Chevy convertibles, knowing that she had loved driving her cars. Granny took one last look at the garage and turned around with a spark in her eye and a look of determination on her face. "Neil Nail did not do this. He would not do this, especially to me. He would not hurt me. I don't know where he is, but I am going to find him and I am going to prove all of you wrong." With that, she turned and walked up the steps onto her porch, turned around and gave her garage one last look, saluted the firemen who were still left and walked into her house, followed by Baskerville who had appeared again out of nowhere.

Franklin turned to the group. "If Hermiony won't let the police protect her, it is up to us. Thor you take the first watch from your window. George, Mavis, the second watch is yours while Thor is sleeping. I'll take over during the day since she would kick me out if I tried to stay the night."

"We'll keep her safe, Franklin," Mavis remarked as George took her arm to escort her back home."

"This should be interesting," Thor warned. "Remember who we are dealing with here. This is my mother; she's cunning and crafty and she would ditch us quicker than we can blink our eyes. Remember that."

Granny watched from her window at the little powwow in her yard. As they all dispersed to go their houses, Franklin to his car, and the Big Guy and police to their station, Granny turned to Baskerville with a smile. "I wonder if they remember my door to the underground street. We might have to test that theory in the morning, Baskerville." As she said those words, her cell phone rang. Granny picked it up to see Franklin on eye to eye. "Yes!" Granny answered in a crusty tone.

"Just thought you might want to know, I picked up the shysters on their way back to your house. They must have been confused when I wasn't home during their time at my house. I'm taking them back home with me. And Granny, I'm watching you." Franklin gave a chuckle and hung up the phone.

The time on Granny's cell phone said 5:00 a.m. The fire took up most of the night. It was time to get a few hours shut eye before she decided to put her plan into place.

CHAPTER TWENTY

The first thing that hit Granny before she even opened her eyes was the smell from the previous night's fire. Not only was it lingering in her house but as she opened her eyes slowly, she saw that she had fallen asleep in her clothes that also smelled like smoke. As she was contemplating her escape in the underground street, she heard someone in her house. She could tell by the female voices that were coming from down the hallway, that her daughters had arrived. Granny wondered why Thor had called them.

A knock sounded on Granny's door. Starshine peeked her head in the door. "Good morning, Mom. Your daughters to the rescue again. We heard about the fire on the news."

Penelope pushed her way through the door past Starshine. "You should have called us. Anyway, that's neither here nor there because we are here now. We hired the Smoke Cleaners to get all this smell out of your house. We got the Wrecking Crew to take care of your garage. And Thor's going to fix your window."

"Uh, you didn't have to do that. I thought I would just rest today. You know, alone, with no one here, didn't get much sleep last night."

"That's the surprise," Starshine gleefully announced. "We're sending you to Shea Fluffallure for a day of rest and a spa treatment."

Granny looked at them in horror. "A spa? One of those fluffy duffy things where they do weird things to you?"

"You'll love it," Penelope assured her. "Imagine that you're a movie star and you are getting ready for your big premiere."

At the words *premiere* and *movie star,* Granny's eyes lit up. "I don't have a car. I can call Mavis. She might drive me."

Granny called Mavis and made arrangements for them to meet on the front lawn in 30 minutes. "You two run along into the kitchen and make yourself some tea," said Granny to her daughters. "I have to freshen up before they spa me." As the two girls turned to go down the hall into the kitchen, Granny closed the bedroom door and gave the lock a turn. She quickly scouted out her room for her flamboyant nightly attire, her reading material that she didn't think her kids would approve of, her chocolates that she stashed under the bed and all her flip flops that she had hidden in various places to keep her kids from confiscating them. She opened the secret door in the back of her closet and threw her stash into the space. After she closed the door, she made her way down the hallway into the bathroom and took a shower to wash off the smoke smell.

Donning her Granny attire, she made sure she also grabbed her pink cane. She might need it where she was going. "I'm ready for the fluffy duffy things," she yelled to her daughters. "It was so sweet of you to do that for me. Mavis is out front so we will see you later."

She was on the way down the steps when she met Thor going up the steps. He looked at Granny. "Oh, no, I see mischief in your eye. You are going to the spa, aren't you? Remember your life is in danger."

Granny looked straight back at Thor. "So is yours if you keep hanging around with that hussy." She tapped Thor lightly on the ankle with her cane and proceeded down the steps and into Mavis' car.

"We're off to Shea Fluffallure to drop you off for a day of beauty. Hold on to your seat belt," Mavis warned as she started the car.

"Ah, Mavis, you have been such a good friend that I think you should take the day at Shea Fluffallure. They told me I would feel like a movie star and since you like to pretend you are in reality TV, you could pretend you are a movie star. Wouldn't that be fun?" Granny suggested.

"And what would you be doing?"

"This fire shook me up so much and everyone's watching me now. I need some alone time. You know how that is, Mavis. You run over to Allure to Shea Fluffallure and use my name. It'll be ok. Stop the car right over here by Rack's. I'll hang out at Esmeralda's old house. No one's there right now. Maybe Neil Nail will come home and I'll be able to talk to him with no one watching."

"I'm supposed to be watching you too," Mavis reminded Granny as she stopped the car.

"Watch," Granny said as she got out of the car and started walking across the street to Esmeralda Periwinkle's old house. "Watch me walk all the way to the back so I can get in the house. Pick me back up at 5:00 p.m. sharp. I'll be here and waiting."

Granny walked to the back of the house making sure no one else was watching her. Mavis pulled away to go to Granny's day of beauty. She knew something that Granny's children didn't. Once Granny made up her mind to do something, there was no talking her out of it. You might just as well let her loose and let the chips fall where they may and hope those chips weren't Granny.

Granny tried the door at the back of the house, but it was locked. She tried picking the lock with her bobby pin but it didn't work and the bobby pin dropped to the ground. As she leaned down to pick it up, she saw that the basement window was now cracked open. Granny wasn't very big so she thought that maybe she could crawl in the window if there was something for her to stand on, on the other side.

Granny went down to the ground and pushed the window open. She used her pink giant knitting needle cane to push it open farther and then stuck her head inside. There was a chair right underneath the window. Granny turned around and, feet first, hoisted herself through the window and down to the chair. This was better yet. If the doors were locked and anyone checked, they would think no one was here. She closed the window all the way just in case.

Once inside, Granny looked around at the basement. It appeared to be as it was the last time she was here. She would start her snooping upstairs.

Once in the kitchen, Granny remembered she was hungry. She hadn't taken time to eat anything. She wondered if there was anything to snack on in the fridge. Certainly Neil must have stocked the fridge. He had. It was full of soda, pickles, sandwich meat that had been bought recently and fresh fruit. There were no donuts and no chocolate. Granny grabbed a couple of grapes to keep her going until she could get something more substantial.

Neil hadn't changed anything in the house but he apparently planned on eating here. Why would he disappear right after he stocked the fridge? Maybe the Big Guy was right and Neil did start the hardware store on fire.

It took Granny a good part of the day to go through the drawers and papers, in the house, but she didn't find anything that indicated Neil lived here. It was also strange that Esmeralda's family hadn't cleaned out the house after she died and before they sold her house.

Perhaps she didn't have any family. Granny decided she needed to check records at the court house to see who her next of kin were. Granny was about to head into the basement when her cell phone rang the *Dragnet* theme.

Before she picked up the phone to do eye to eye, Granny ran into the bathroom, soaked a towel, ran into the bedroom and lay on the bed and plopped the towel around her face so you could only see her eyes. She then answered her phone.

"Franklin, don't you know you aren't supposed to disturb me when I am spa-ing? I'm trying to relax," Granny shouted through the towel.

"Just checking on you to see if you were having a good time; can't get Mavis on the phone so I was thinking you two might be in trouble."

"She was going to a movie, while I got *spa tee da'd*. Probably has her phone off. Gotta go, my bikini wax is next." Granny knew she heard that they did those sometimes at the spa although she had no idea what they were.

"Meet me at Rack's at 5:00. I've got news." Franklin clicked off of eye to eye and hung up. Granny threw the towel to the floor. She was running out of time to find out what happened to Esmeralda and to Neil. Deciding she needed to check the yard and the garage, she tromped back down into the basement to climb out the window. As she was walking in the dark past the cut in the wall, she noticed a little light shining through the cut. Quietly, she walked over to the wall and put her eye to the very slight cut. All she could see was a sliver of light. She could hear no sound. Granny looked around for something to cut more of the wall when she heard a pounding on the outside door. She quickly moved away from the wall and over to the basement window, climbing on the chair so she could see who was there. It was Mavis

Granny pushed the window open and whispered, "Mavis, Mavis, be quiet." When Mavis kept pounding, Granny took her knitting needle cane that she was holding on to, took the end off and poked it out the window. It was long enough to reach Mavis and poke her in the foot lightly.

"Ow." Mavis looked down and grabbed her foot. She saw Granny. "What are you doing?"

"What are you doing raising a ruckus? Remember, no one is supposed to know we're here."

"Franklin called. He's meeting us at 5:00. It's 4:30."

"So? Rack's is right across the street."

"He's expecting you to be spa'd. Have you looked at yourself? You don't look any different than when you left your house this morning." Mavis peered down at Granny. "Well, I take that back, you look worse."

"We'll just tell him the spa treatment failed. I told him I got a bikini wax, whatever that is, but I think it's something he can't see, kind of like a hidden tattoo. It'll keep him wondering." Granny laughed in glee at the thought.

"Get up here and open this door," retorted Mavis. "I went shopping after my day at the spa. I got you some clothes that I thought looked like you and some new pins for your hair and some make up! I don't star in my own imaginary reality shows for nothing."

Granny trudged up the steps and let Mavis in the back door. They made sure they didn't turn on any lights. Granny led Mavis to the big pantry that Esmeralda had. There were no windows in there to give off light.

Mavis dumped out the bags she was carrying. "Let's do the makeup first so we don't get your clothes messed." She grabbed foundation, mascara and bright blue eye shadow and started plopping them on Granny's face.

"Can I look?"

"Not yet. An artist doesn't let you see the final product until it is done." Mavis almost poked Granny in the eye with the mascara as she decorated Granny's eyes.

"Here's your dress; put it on."

Granny looked at the bright red silk dress that was straight and form-fitting with a little flare at the bottom. "I thought it would go great with your red sparkly high tops," Mavis explained, "Now your hair." Mavis twirled Granny around and put her long hair down and fastened the sides of her hair with the new red rhinestone clips. She then plopped a new red wide brimmed hat on Granny's head

"Just in case I screwed up the makeup, no one will see your face so they won't know you haven't been to the spa. And when you are asked, just say that it was delightful, You can't find the words to describe it."

Granny turned and looked at Mavis with new respect. "Why, Mavis, this is a side of you I haven't seen before. I think I like it. Deception becomes you."

"We have to go; no time to look in the mirror. Let me out, go back down and come out the basement window and no one will be the wiser that we were here."

With the door locked after Mavis' departure to the outside, Granny made her way down the steps, noticing on her way to the window that there was no longer light shining through the crack in the wall. That was something she was going to have to investigate later.

Mavis was waiting at the window and as Granny put the chair back under the window; Mavis lifted the window out as wide as it would open so Granny could crawl through the window. She helped Granny through the window, trying to keep Granny from getting her dress caught or her hair mussed. Once Granny made it through the window and was back up on her feet, the two women carefully made their way around the side of house making sure no one was watching. After seeing that the coast was clear, they hustled their way across the street to Rack's restaurant's parking lot. They hadn't counted on the fact that Franklin would be sitting in Granny's booth by the window. Both women stopped on a dime when they realized Franklin was staring out of the window at them. He said something to someone across the table in the booth. Mavis paled a little under her makeup when she realized George had accompanied Franklin to Rack's.

"What do we do now, Granny? They saw us?"

Granny patted Mavis' hand and took her by the arm and proceeded to enter the door to Rack's restaurant. "Follow my lead, Mavis."

As they approached the booth, Granny turned to Mavis. "Yes, Mrs. Periwinkle's house might be the perfect house for your friend from Allure. It is very quaint and cute. Hi, Franklin. George, I didn't know that you were going to join us," Granny said innocently.

"What were you doing at Neil Nail's house?" Franklin asked Granny in a suspicious voice.

"Well, you see Mavis met an old friend in Allure and she is thinking about moving to Fuchsia, so we thought we would walk around Esmeralda's house. Neil didn't live there long enough for it to be called his house. We thought we would walk around it, look at it and see if it would work for her."

Mavis stammered, "Ah, and it would. It would."

"Mavis, you look like you have been at a movie star premiere reality show. You look beautiful," George said adoringly, while gazing at Mavis.

"Don't I look good too, Franklin? Mavis decided to spend some time at the spa too?" Granny made a pirouette around her cane.

Franklin peered at Granny giving her a close look. "You look pretty good too, I must admit. I was suspicious whether you would make it to the spa. That is why we sent Mavis to keep an eye on you. Mavis, good job, you kept her out of trouble."

Mavis started squirming in her seat, never being very good at subterfuge. Just in time, the waitress brought their drinks to their table, saving Mavis from answering. After they had ordered, Franklin cleared his throat.

"I have news. Neil Nail has disappeared. The APB has garnered no leads. The Big Guy has checked out Neil's father's death a little further. It appears that Neil is the one behind the poisoning and murder of Sally and Esmeralda Periwinkle. His father became suspicious so Neil had to see that his father wouldn't talk to the police."

"I was there when Mr. Nail died. I was the one to find him. Neil didn't have anything to do with it," Granny reminded them.

"The shelves had been tampered with, Granny. All Mr. Nail had to do was to get a bag off the shelf and that would have triggered the weakness in the shelf to bring down all the shelves and fertilizer on top of whoever tried to take the bag down, and since Mr. Nail was the only one who sold the fertilizer that would make him the target."

"Couldn't it have been someone else?" Mavis asked.

"We tested the bags. The bags on the right on the shelves were tainted with a little known fast growing weed seed. And then there is the lavender tea that Mr. Nail gave to the women when they bought the fertilizer. There is also the fact that Neil was very nervous and set those fires before he disappeared. He was trying to get rid of evidence."

"But why start my garage on fire? It doesn't make sense," Granny interjected.

"Don't take this the wrong way, but you are a snoop and something you must have found must have worried him," Franklin answered.

Mavis and George both eyed Granny, wondering how she was going to take being called a snoop by Franklin, but it appeared that Granny had other things on her mind. Her gaze was focused on the front of the restaurant. Thor and Elena had just arrived.

"What does he see in that woman? I don't trust her."

"Hermiony, she's a beautiful young woman. Any man Thor's age or older would give her a second look," Franklin suggested as he too watched as Thor and Elena were seated at a table towards the front of the restaurant."

"He's right, Granny; she is a looker," George interjected.

"I think it's time we go home, George," Mavis said as she started pushing him out of the booth.

"We haven't eaten yet. We just ordered," George protested. "

I think I'll go with you. This spa-ing adventure has been a tiring day and, besides, I want to make sure my kids left my house in one piece. Since Thor's here that must mean the girls are done or he left them to their own devices to finish my house and that's an even scarier thought than Thor being here with that hussy. Perhaps, since you are an older man, emphasis on *older,* Franklin, and you think she deserves a second look, perhaps you should give her one," Granny advised in a huffy tone. She gave Franklin a nudge so he would let her out of the booth.

"On second thought, George, perhaps you should sit back down." Mavis gave George a push back into the booth. He lost his balance and sat down. Since she's such a looker, perhaps you should look. I'll give Granny a ride home. You two enjoy your meal." Mavis winked at Granny and the two of them ambled toward the door, walking past the booth with Thor and Elena. Granny couldn't resist giving Thor a little tap on the leg with her cane as she walked by.

As they were getting into Mavis' car, Mavis turned to Granny, "Now what?"

"We're going home," Granny said innocently.

"That's it, straight home? Are you sure? I'm having fun helping you with your snooping."

"Now, Mavis, I do not snoop. I care, that is all. I care. I am going home to see the shysters and Baskerville. I am going to grab my wine, chocolate and settle into bed with a good book and make sure my house is all in one piece."

Mavis let Granny out in front of Granny's house. Granny looked to where the garage had been. The garage was gone, torn down and all that was left in its place was the cement floor that used to support Granny's garage. Granny gave a sigh, mourning her cars and wondering what she was going to do without a car. Perhaps she could rent one until she could buy a new one. Waving to Mavis, she let herself in her house.

A circus greeted Granny when she opened the door to the house. Mr. Bleaty was back and the shysters weren't happy as Mr. Bleaty was trying to keep them from their food. Baskerville was guarding Mr. Bleaty. The situation appeared to be out of hand. Granny reached into the corner and grabbed her umbrella. With one slip of the crook, she managed to capture the collar on Mr. Bleaty. Leading him by her umbrella and ignoring Baskerville's loud howl of protest, she led Mr.

Bleaty outside and over to Sally's old house. Baskerville was still howling and following the two of them. The shysters didn't follow, too busy eating after being kept from their food by Mr. Bleaty.

Granny led Mr. Bleaty to the garage. The door was standing wide open and so was the gate to his pen. Granny led him inside of the garage and put him in the pen and slammed it shut, making sure the latch was securely latched. She turned to Baskerville. "Home," she said sternly as she pointed in the direction of her house. Baskerville looked at Granny and walked over to Mr. Bleaty's pen, reached his nose across the fence and gave Mr. Bleaty a nudge before turning around and walking out the door. Granny followed Baskerville and shut the door to the garage hearing the lock click as the door closed.

Granny watched as Baskerville trotted home, heard his howl so the door would open and he could get in the house. She then took time to survey the yard. The hussy was with Thor at Rack's and it looked like Mavis had already turned in for the night. Granny pulled out her Itphone and activated the flashlight feature. She trained the flashlight on the cistern that was still hidden by the dying weeds.

Walking over to the cistern, she shone the flashlight around the edges of the cover. All of a sudden her nose started twitching and she started sneezing. What was that smell? Whatever it was, it was coming from the cistern and it was a smell Granny hadn't encountered before. She tried to move the lid off of the cistern but it wouldn't budge.

Granny started walking toward the house to go back home when she looked overhead and saw the stars twinkling brightly in the night. The cool frosty air seemed to make the stars pop out like diamonds in the sky. It was dark all around her.

Granny started thinking about Sally and took a few minutes to sit down in the middle of the yard on the cool earth of fall. Thoughts of Sally ran through her head, remembering their times together, although they were quirky moments. Granny remembered them fondly. On a whim, she lay down on the ground remembering Sally on the ground with her ear to the ground saying, "The grass is a living thing. The grass talks to me." Granny lay down on the ground in the darkness and looked up at the sky. She closed her eyes for a minute when she heard what sounded like whispering or talking coming from the ground. Granny sat up and looked around. There was no one around her. She put her ear to the ground and again she heard what she thought was talking. Was Sally right? Did she have magical grass that talked? But there was no grass now, just weeds. Granny lay back down and listened but everything was silent. Maybe she had imagined it because she was thinking of Sally. It was time to go home and visit with the shysters and head to bed. Granny tapped on George and Mavis' bedroom window as she walked by their house. *They may not be wed but at least they're not dead.* Granny thought and then she chuckled at her rhyme.

CHAPTER TWENTY-ONE

The thunder was crashing over Granny's head as the lightning split a tree next to her garage and flames erupted, shooting tentacles of fire at her garage. Standing in the pouring rain, Granny watched as the lightning also shot through the window of the garage and hit both gas tanks of her two red '57 Chevy Corvettes simultaneously. They exploded, erupting into words shooting up into the sky. The words scrolled above her head as the rain parted letting the words form into perfect letters of fire. Granny could see what the fire was trying to tell her. The words swarmed in flame over her head. "The grass quit talking to me, the grass quit talking to me, the grass quit talking to me." Granny yelled at the flames, "You killed her! You killed her!" The flames turned into blades of grass, which quickly turned into weeds, and the weeds started swirling to the ground.

At that moment, Granny rolled over in bed and fell out of the bed swiftly onto the floor encased in a roll of her blankets. As she groggily awoke from the dream she heard loud pounding on her door and the doorbell ringing.

Granny reached for her Itphone to see what time it was. *Who was pounding on her door at 6:00 a.m.?* Granny grabbed the bedpost and the mattress and hoisted herself up off the floor as the pounding and doorbell ringing continued. She grabbed her cane for protection and threw on her new robe that was covered with pictures of her shysters and cautiously walked down the hall to the front door. The shysters and Baskerville didn't seem to be around. Granny wondered where her bodyguards were when she needed them.

Before answering the pounding, she peeked out the side window to see who might be disturbing her so early. When she saw who it was she threw open the door. "What do you want? Do you know it's only 6:00 a.m.?"

"Where are they? Where are they?" The hussy shouted.

"Who are you talking about?"

"Gottlieb and that monster mutt of yours."

"I'm sure Baskerville is with the shysters at Franklin's. I have no idea where Mr. Bleaty is. Last I saw him, he was in the pen in your garage. He broke into my house last night and terrorized my shysters. I took him back to his home and locked the gate and the garage since you left them open in your haste to schmooze my son."

"I closed those doors. Your mutt opened them like he did this morning. I saw them running over here."

"They're not here. I would have heard Baskerville howl if they would have come in. Go ahead look around." Granny swept her arms wide indicating a free search for Elena.

Just as Elena was going to search Granny's bedroom, they heard a noise in the basement. Elena changed direction and charged down the steps with Granny at her heels.

"There, there. You lied! You said they weren't here! Wait until I tell Thor that his mother kidnapped my goat and then tried to hide him from me."

Granny stood open-mouthed for a minute, too shocked to answer as she looked at the hidden fireplace door that was standing open. She forgot about Elena, Mr. Bleaty and Baskerville as she walked through the door to the underground room connecting to the streets of Fuchsia. The door to the underground street was open. *Had she left it open and forgotten?*

Granny turned back into her family room after closing and locking both doors. Deep in thought, she almost forgot that the hussy was still there.

"I should call the cops and have you arrested for goat napping." Elena spit at her.

"You opened that door, didn't you? And then you came in here to accuse me of goat napping. You're conspiring against me to get rid of me so you can get your hooks into my son."

"I already have my hooks into your son and there's not anything you can do about it. Once I tell him his poor mom is wandering around in yards at night and imagining locking doors and garage doors, he'll send you to the wrinkle farm."

Granny skewered up her eyes. She still had her cane in her hand and thought about flicking off the tip and using it on the hussy. Before she could reply to the hussy's threat, they heard a knock on the door. Granny thought that early morning was becoming very busy around this neighborhood recently.

"Mom, mom, are you ok?"

Elena glared at Granny and called out, "We're down here, Thor!"

Thor came down the steps and eyed the two women cautiously. "Mavis was hanging upside down in her exercise bed when she heard some noise over here. Said she thought it sounded like someone was trying to break in so she called me to check on you, Mom."

Elena walked over to Thor and threw her arms around his neck and plastered her face into his shoulder, feigning tears. "It was me, Honey. Her bruiser of a dog grabbed Gottlieb and was going to hurt him. He brought him over here and I came over to try to rescue him. I found them here in the basement. Your mother is very confused and she was going to attack me with her cane. I don't think she knows who I am. She keeps calling me someone called the hussy." Elena peeked out at Granny from her position on Thor's chest.

Granny couldn't believe the words coming out of Elena's mouth. Before Granny could protest, Elena swooned and fainted. Thor lifted her up in his arms and started to carry her up the stairs, but not before turning to Granny. "We will talk about his later; please see that Gottlieb gets home. I'm taking her to the ER to make sure she is ok. Really, Mom, attacking Elena?" As Thor was looking at Granny, Elena opened her eyes and winked at Granny as Thor carried her up the stairs. Granny heard Thor talking to the hussy.

"Sweetheart, you are going to be fine. I'll see to it and I will see my mother never treats you that way ever again."

Granny heard voices upstairs as Thor was leaving. Mavis came down the steps. "Are you ok? We saw Elena trying to break down your door. That's why we called Thor."

"Who, Elena attacking my door?" Granny said in a sweet voice and then she dropped to the floor in a pretend swoon. "Oh, Thor," Granny said, mimicking Elena, "Your mother attacked me, you have to put her away."

Mavis stared at Granny wide eyed. "She said that?"

"Not in so many words," Granny said gruffly, standing back up. "She's a fake and she wants my son and she's not gonna get him. Over my dead body is she going to get my son. I think I need to have a dinner party."

"Ah, Granny? A dinner party? Ah, you don't really cook very well. Who are you going to poison? Elena?" Mavis asked suspiciously.

"Mavis, will you take Mr. Bleaty back? I have to get to town and talk to the Big Guy."

"It's kind of cold to walk Granny and it is very early. Why don't you wait, and George and I will drive you."

"I'm a Fuchsia, Minnesotan. I know you wouldn't understand that because you're from outside of Fuchsia. But we Fusciasotans are tough. Besides, I want to stop and talk to that Heather on the way to town too. Go, go, go," Granny urged as she shooed Mavis and Mr. Bleaty upstairs and out the door, leaving Baskerville sulking in the basement at the loss of his friend.

It was a little too early to head to town. Granny thought she might make the rounds of the stores when she got there and see if there were any pilferers grabbing the goods in the store. She knew the Big Guy thought she was in danger but who would hurt a little Granny in the middle of a Fuchsia store?

Baskerville finally decided to come back upstairs. Granny felt sorry for him so she opened the door to her fridge and got him some ice cream and a donut. It looked so good she decided to join Baskerville and have some too. She also made herself some coffee to dunk her donut. It would keep her awake since she was up so early. Her eyes still felt like they needed toothpicks to hold them up. She hadn't been able to wake slowly as was her normal routine.

Granny looked at Baskerville. "Why aren't you following the shysters these days, Baskerville? I'm sure they miss you."

Baskerville finished his ice cream and donut and walked over and put his head in Granny's lap. A soft moan came out of his body.

"Oh, Baskerville, are you in love with Mr. Bleaty? He might be bad news just like his owner. Maybe this is a rebound love since you lost your other home not too long ago. We'll work on this." Granny patted the top of his head and gently moved it off her lap so she could go to her bedroom to get dressed in her Granny disguise.

As Granny pulled on her polyester skirt and hose, she remembered she had meant to buy a new coat for the fall but hadn't gotten around to it yet. Then she remembered she still had Sally's bright green jacket in her closet. It wasn't pink or fuchsia but maybe wearing the green jacket that had been Sally's would spark something that would make her closer to finding the killer in Fuchsia. Granny couldn't believe Neil Nail had it in him.

Granny grabbed the jacket and her pink cane. They made a stunning combination. As Granny opened the door to step outside, she realized that it was pretty cool and it looked like it could rain or sleet again. Going back into her house, Granny walked downstairs and unlatched the fireplace door. She also unlatched the door going into the underground streets. She would walk back that way and see if there was any progress being made at opening them to the public. After all, the mayor had promised they would be open by the Christmas shopping season.

On her way back upstairs, Granny put her hand into the pocket of the coat. *What in the world? Weeds? What was Sally doing with weeds in her pocket?*

Granny emptied her pocket of the weeds and dumped them in her trash can that was in the kitchen. Baskerville was sitting by the door and opted to follow Granny out the door. Once they were on the front sidewalk, Baskerville started to cross the street to the hussy's house.

"Baskerville, no! Come with me, lets go see Angel." Baskerville halted for a second. Granny thought she was going to have to get tough as it seemed he was going to ignore her command, but at the name 'Angel,' he turned and started after Granny.

As Granny walked, she noticed the Fuchsia Street Department was filling the potholes with leaves and packing them down for the winter. The potholes prevented Fuchsia from having to install rumble strips to remind residents to stop. In the fall they filled the potholes with leaves. The city never gave an explanation why they did this, but it was Fuchsia and there was no reason to question the reason why. It had always been done that way and Fuchsia folks liked the routine. In fact, some years they had a pothole filling contest. The person who could fit the most leaves in a pothole won a night for two at the Lake of the Leaves Bed and Breakfast in Allure.

Granny was so deep in thought that she forgot she was going to stop at Heather's house on the way to town. Baskerville hadn't forgotten and he had been leading. He stopped so fast that Granny tumbled right over him to the ground. When Granny lifted her head off of the ground, she found she was staring at some large black shoes. She looked up to see Franklin's eyes twinkling above her, a long way above her.

"You do like falling for me, don't you Granny?" Franklin chuckled as he helped Granny to her feet. "Are you on your way to town?"

"I am, got woke up early this morning by that hussy. She made such a ruckus it brought Thor over and he hauled her away to the hospital ER."

"What did you do to her?"

"Me? Me?"

"Yes, you. That sweet girl wouldn't hurt a fly."

"Franklin, I always thought I was a good judge of character but maybe not if you and my son can be bamboozled by that woman. I came to talk to your daughter."

Franklin studied Granny with a suspicious look. "Why?"

"I'm having a dinner party. Tonight. You're invited."

"Hermiony, you don't like to cook. Why would you have a dinner party and why would Heather be invited?"

"It's time our families got to know one another. After all, you are my fiancé. It'll be fun. You, me, Heather, Angel and Thor. I'll even invite Starshine and Penelope and Butch. See, nothing to be suspicious about. With all this hoopla, it'll be nice to do something normal," Granny cajoled.

"I don't know if I would call you putting on a dinner party normal. But at least it'll keep you out of trouble. I tell you what. I'll invite Heather and I'll even run over to the hospital and check on Thor and Elena. I'll invite Thor for you. That way you can concentrate on your cooking."

"No Elena, you hear. No hussy. No floozy," Granny instructed as she pointed her finger at Franklin.

"Relax. I won't invite her, although it would be a neighborly thing to do."

Granny stomped her cane on the ground. Franklin started laughing a big belly laugh.

"Just teasing. Do you need a ride since you don't have a car to carry the groceries and it looks like it is going to get nasty."

"No," Granny answered. "I have it all taken care of."

Granny looked around for Baskerville. He had taken the time to disappear while Granny was talking to Franklin. Granny hoped he wasn't back visiting Mr. Bleaty.

"Keep an eye out for Baskerville. We don't want him to start bleating instead of howling." Granny winked at Franklin and continued her journey to Main Street. Once she reached Main Street, she realized that she had been going to go and talk to the Big Guy. That was the problem with her memory; it got easily distracted.

Granny decided to stop at AbStract first to scope out the customers. Estelle was back behind the jewelry counter. "Glad to see you're back, Estelle, and none the worse for the wear."

"Me too, Granny, that was a scary experience."

"You learned your lesson, Estelle; sometimes a pretty boy isn't all they're cut out to be. He may be cute, but all he wanted was your loot."

Estelle started laughing. "Granny, I love your rhymes and I will be careful from now on."

Jack Puffleman, owner of AbStract walked up to Granny. "Granny, can I talk to you a minute?"

"Sure, Jack, I wanted to show you my new weapon so you'll feel safe if you don't see my umbrella." Granny led Jack into the corner where she had first fallen into the underground streets. Granny looked around at the changes.

"Why, lookee here. You can get to the underground from here. You made it a real door." Granny started to open the door when Puffleman stopped her.

"You can check that out later, Granny. The City Council is building access to all the stores that connect to the streets but now I need to talk to you."

Granny raised her cane in the air. "This is what I wanted to show you. Look, it is a giant knitting needle disguised as a cane. I will be able to skewer a scoundrel with the jab of a swordsman." Granny jumped into skewering mode, holding her giant knitting needle in front of her. With one jab she skewered the mannequin in the aisle. One poke and the mannequin went falling to the floor. Granny pulled out her knitting needle. With a look of triumph she said, "I might have to work on that jab. Don't want to skewer anybody dead, just want to poke them so the Big Guy can put them in the pokey." With the play on words, Granny started laughing until she noticed Jack Puffleman wasn't doing the same.

"What's the matter, Jack? I won't skewer you," Granny reassured him.

"Um, um," Jack Puffleman said nervously. "I don't know how to break this to you, Granny, but you can't sleuth for us anymore. The Big Guy says your life is in danger and we can't put you at risk until the perpetrator is caught."

"The who? The what? Perculator? Sorry, I can't hear you." Granny put the end back on her giant knitting needle and turned and walked out the door.

The police station was next to the fire station. Granny made a beeline for the station looking for the Big Guy.

"Hey, Granny," Ned Nifflemeyer, one of the patrolmen for Fuchsia, greeted her as she stomped in the door.

"The Big Guy. I need the Big Guy."

"He's out, Granny."

"Where is he?"

"I am not supposed to reveal that information," Ned said in a serious tone.

Granny took her cane and banged it on the desk.

"Sorry, Granny, your scare tactics will not get me to reveal his whereabouts," Ned said as he stood up and crossed his arms over his chest.

Granny gave him a stubborn look and then collapsed in the chair in front of the desk. "Oh, Ned, there has been another attempt on my life. I was attacked by someone named Miss Hussy. And she wasn't alone. Mr. Bleaty helped her. Please," Granny sniffed, "I have to talk to him."

Ned handed Granny a tissue. Granny hid her eyes. "Sorry, Granny. I didn't know. He'd want to know.

He's next door at the firehouse at Ella's makeshift coffee house having coffee and a donut."

"What! He's next door and you couldn't tell me that! I'll have your badge for obstructing my justice over a coffee and a donut!" Granny pointed her cane-covered knitting needle at his chest. "You are so lucky that I didn't decide to knit you a new hole in your shirt."

Granny stood up, hit the cane on the desk and proceeded outside and next door to the fire hall to find the Big Guy. Besides, Granny also need to talk to Delight about food for her dinner party.

Granny slowed down as she walked in the door, leaning on her cane heavily. With all the firemen and the policeman having such close access to Ella's, it was hard to find a place to sit these days because the place was always full unless there was a fire or a big crime spree. Granny did notice that the waists of the firemen and policemen seemed to be getting a little bigger the past few weeks.

Granny spied the Big Guy over in the corner. She shuffled her way to the table.

"Moving a little slow today, aren't you, Granny?"

"I was attacked in my own house this morning. It slowed me down a little."

The word *attacked* got the Big Guy's attention. He stood up and held the chair for Granny to sit down. Delight, seeing that Granny had come in, brought her a cup of Boneyard Specialty Blend coffee and a double donut with chocolate and crème filling in between the two donuts. It was topped with more chocolate, raspberries and whipped crème.

"Thank you, Delight. I don't believe I've had this donut before. The raspberry touch is a nice new addition," Granny remarked as she sipped her coffee.

"It is my little way of making my desserts healthy," Delight explained. "I have heard raspberries are very good for you and I want my customers to be healthy."

"Give me a minute with the Big Guy and then I need your creativity." Granny winked at Delight so Delight would give her a minute with the Big Guy.

The Big Guy watched Delight walk away before turning his attention to Granny. "What happened?"

"That hussy across the street from me broke into my house this morning, threatened me and siced her goat on me. I want you to arrest her. Besides, I know she had something to do with Sally's murder."

The Big Guy looked at Granny thoughtfully. "And you know this how?"

"She's remodeling her basement. There is a cut in the wall. Maybe she buried something. And...her weeds talk. And Sally didn't have any daughters."

"Do you have any witnesses to this attack?"

"Mavis and George and Thor," Granny said emphatically.

"And if I questioned them, would they back up your story?"

"Well, maybe. But what I am telling you is true. Something is going on over there. You need to look into it before more people die."

The Big Guy heaved a big sigh, grabbed Granny's cane before speaking so that he would not get jabbed in one of her wild spurts of energy and replied, "The case is almost closed. As soon as we find Neil Nail, we will be able to arrest him and close it. He killed the two women and he started the fires and there is the possibility that he killed his father too."

"He wouldn't do that. I have another bone to pick with you. Jack Puffleman won't let me work undercover in his store anymore and he said the merchants have orders from you." Granny poked her finger directly at the Big Guy.

Another big sigh came out of the Big Guy. "Until we catch Neal Nail, your life is in danger. You know something but you don't know what it is. The sad thing is that whatever you know you have probably forgotten, never to be remembered again and Neil doesn't know that."

"Well when I remember what I've forgotten that, according to you, I will never remember again I will forget to tell you," Granny said with a smug grin as she got up and went find Delight.

CHAPTER TWENTY-TWO

The table was ready. The shysters and Baskerville were locked in her bedroom. The food was being kept warm in the oven. Granny had decided on stuffed chicken breast with roasted potatoes, grilled asparagus and a side salad of fruit topped with honey apple dressing. Her chocolate, peanut butter cup cheesecake was cooling in her second fridge in the basement and as an appetizer Granny had seared duck livers with roasted scallops and curried cauliflower puree. The scene was set.

Granny pulled out her pots and pans from the drawers and opened a can of chicken broth and dumped it over the pans. She then took her pans and rinsed them in the sink and put them in the dish drain. After doing that, she pulled out her chicken-scented room spray and spritzed it around the room. She put her nose up in the air and sniffed. Yes, it smell like cooked chicken. When she was sure that it smelled like she had cooked the foo, she hid the spray and pulled out a fuchsia apron with a large coffee cup on the front and put it on. Then she went over to the drawer and pulled out the flour and fluffed a little on her apron.

Granny looked down. Yes, it looked like she had been cooking. Thank goodness for the underground streets today. Not only had it been sleeting when Granny had left Ella's Enchanted Forest at the Fire Hall but she needed a way for Delight to deliver the food without anyone seeing her. Mission accomplished.

Granny lifted up the top of the foot stool and moved the blanket inside, opening the bottom to grab her bottle of wine and a glass and poured herself a small glass of wine as she waited for her guests. She thought this was a pretty good idea if she hadn't said so herself.

The doorbell rang as Granny was drinking her last drop of wine. She quickly threw the glass underneath the blanket inside the footstool and answered the door. The smiling faces of her daughters greeted her.

"This is so much fun, Mother," Penelope stated as she handed her mom a plant and moved inside the house.

"May the stars line up perfectly for you tonight, Mother," Starshine said as she kissed Granny on the cheek.

Granny looked at the plant, wondering how she was going to keep it alive until summer. She might have to get a few pointers from Delight and Ella on how they kept their forest alive all these years.

Both girls look at Granny expectantly. "What's the occasion?"

"No occasion," replied Granny. "Can't a body have a dinner party? Where's Butch?" she added, referring to Penelope's husband and changing the subject.

"He said he couldn't take any more drama today. He had a bad day at work," said Penelope. "Some woman from Fuchsia came to our town looking for a yard alarm and since he is in the alarm business someone sent her to Butch,." Penelope explained. "Well this woman said she had a nosy old neighbor who kept stealing her goat and she wanted her stopped. Well, Butch said to her, 'She's getting your goat, eh?' and this woman started yelling and attacking Butch. His boss came out and the woman started to turn sweet as pie. As a result, Butch was suspended for a couple of days because the woman fainted and had to be taken to the ER. Short story long, he couldn't take any of our family dramatics tonight. You don't happen to know who that woman was and who the old woman was who she was talking about do you, Mom?"

At that moment, the doorbell rang again. Granny hurried to the door so she didn't have to answer Penelope. It couldn't have been the hussy anyway, or if it was, at least Granny was warned.

Franklin, Heather and Angel stepped into the house. Angel ran up to Granny and hugged her tight. "I love you, my new Granny."

Granny knelt down and gave Angel a hug.

"Where is Baskerville? Where are Itsy and Bitsy and Fish and Little White Poodle?" Angel asked innocently. "I want to play with them."

At that moment, the door opened aagain and Thor walked into the room. Granny decided it was time for introductions. "Penelope, Starshine, meet Heather and Angel. Heather is one of Franklin's daughters". Granny was about to introduce Thor and Heather when Thor said, "We've already met." He walked to the far side of the room, ignoring Heather and winking at Angel.

This wasn't going quite as planned, Granny thought to herself.

"Mother, do you still have Baskerville?" Starshine asked in a soft voice. "I just loved him."

Angel piped up. "Me too and I love my Grandpa's Itsy and Bitsy and my new almost Grandma's Little White Poodle and Fish."

Starshine and Penelope turned to look at Granny. Granny started to answer but Franklin stepped in and said, "Well, you see Fish was rescued from the pet store and Little White Poodle needed a home so Granny graciously took them in. Itsy and Bitsy are mine and when the four met they became inseparable. We share custody so there is nothing for you to worry about. And

Baskerville adopted both of us. With your mother being so frail," (The word *frail* coming out of Franklin's mouth stiffened Granny's spine) "a few pets to look after her and keep her moving are just what she needs. She needs a reason to get out of bed in the morning," Franklin said with a twinkle in his eye.

"Yes," Granny piped up in a crotchety voice while peering at Franklin. "Pets are just what I need to put a little bite in my bark. They'll protect me from old letcherous men who attack me. Time to eat; everyone, sit down. Thor, I have a place for you right next to Heather. Franklin, you can sit on one side of Angel and I will sit on the other. Penelope and Starshine, take your places on any of the three chairs. I had a place set for Butch but that's ok."

Franklin chimed in, "You could invite Elena."

Granny ignored Franklin as she set each plate of appetizers in front of each person. All eyes looked to the plate. Granny's children all looked at each other. "Ah, Mom, what might this be?" Thor asked.

"It is my specialty and it is a surprise." At that moment, the doorbell rang. "Eat, I'll get the door," Granny instructed the diners.

Reluctantly, they put fork to the plate but could not quite bring it to their mouths.

Granny opened the door to find the Big Guy. "I need to talk to you, Granny."

"Cornelius, come on in."

The Big Guy cautiously stepped into the house. "I didn't realize it was mealtime. I'll come back."

"No," Thor, Starshine and Penelope chimed in at once.

"Sit down," Thor said, "My mother's meals are notoriously well known for their creativity. My brother-in-law couldn't make it and we have more food than we can eat." Thor motioned with his hand that the Big Guy should sit down.

Penelope moved over and left a chair in between her and Starshine. The Big Guy sat down. Granny got him a plate of seared duck livers and roasted scallops. He lifted his fork and dug in as everyone watched him take his first bite. Because of his arrival, the others had delayed their taste of the delicacy.

"Granny, this is wonderful. I don't know what it is but it warms my palate. Thanks for the invite."

After skeptical looks, the others took their first bite. Soon the appetizer was gone. "Wow," Starshine said, "Did you go to cooking school when we weren't looking? What's in this?"

"I'll tell ya later. Moving on." Granny got up and grabbed the salad for the next course, not wanting to let them know that they had just wet their appetite on seared duck livers. This time the entire table dug into the food, still cautious but with a little more enthusiasm.

"Why did you stop by, Cornelius? This an official visit? If it is, my meal might be considered bribery."

"Don't worry Granny," said the Big Guy. "I was checking on you to make sure you were ok. I didn't know your entire family and friends would be here. After our last conversation, I decided to stop by to see if you remembered what you forgot."

Angel piped in, "I always forgotted. My mommy says I forgotted to wash my hands and brush my teeth on purpose but I just forgotted cause I was so busy playing with Baskerville and his goat."

All eyes turned to Angel. "Goat? What goat, Angel?" Heather asked her daughter.

"The one that comes to visit with Baskerville. You've never seen him, Mommy, cause he hided when you came out of the house."

"Don't look at me,"Granny protested, "I don't have a goat. It's that hussy across the street and Baskerville seems real taken with her goat."

Franklin turned to Angel and in a soft voice said, "Angel, you shouldn't keep secrets like that from your mommy or me. Ok?"

"I knows. I won't do it again. I'll only keep mommy's secret. Mommy, is it ok if I tell Granny and Grandpa our secret?" Angel asked innocently.

The conversation was interupted by Thor coughing loudly. As he stood up from the table, he knocked the water glass over onto the floor.

"I'm ok, I'm ok. Let me get this cleaned up. What do you have planned for us next, Mother?"

Granny stood and walked to the kitchen, opened the oven and brought out the plates of stuffed chicken breast, roasted potatoes and grilled asparagus and one by one picked them up and set them in front of her guests.

Franklin eyed his plate as Granny sat down to join the group. "I didn't know you could cook like this, Hermiony. You are a gourmet cook. Is there anything you can't do?"

Granny hid a grin, "Why, Franklin, you are just getting a glimpse of my many talents."

After eveyone finished eating, Granny was about to collect their plates when Starshine turned to the Big Guy. "Why are you keeping track of my mother?"

"Yes, I would like to know the same thing," Penelope chimed in. "Thor, what haven't you told us?"

The Big Guy started to look uncomfortable. He stood up. "I, ah, must be going. My phone just beeped in my pocket. Duty calls. Thanks for the dinner, Granny; sorry I am going to miss dessert." He quickly turned, grabbed his coat that was by the door and left.

Franklin turned to Angel. "How about we have dessert in a little while. Why don't I let Baskerville and the shysters out of the bedroom and you take them downstairs to play. Then we can have dessert."

"I'll get them," replied Angel. "I know how to open a door. You won't forget to let me have dessert?"

"We couldn't have dessert without you," her mom assured her.

Angel quickly got up, ran down the hallway and opened Granny's bedroom door. Baskerville bounded out excitedly. He ran over to the table and gave Starshine a big lick on the face. She giggled. The shysters were more cautious, knowing Granny's family was a little persnickity about animals in Granny's house.

"Come on, come on, let's play," Angel called as she started down the steps. Hearing her voice, the shysters and Baskerville followed.

"Now, what don't we know?" Penelope demanded.

"Well, um, it seems someone, um, tried to poison me and then they set my garage on fire."

"What!" Penelope and Starshine said at the same time.

"That's it. You are coming home to live with me or going somewhere where you will be safe," Penelope stated.

"Not the wrinkle farm!" Granny stated in horror.

Starshine shook her head. "No, Mom, you are too young for the wrinkle farm yet, although don't push us," she warned.

"Stop, all of you," Franklin said. "We have this under control. Neil Nail is the one responsible for the murders and for the attacks on Granny. He has disappeared, but we have an APB out on him and as soon as we nail him," Franklin chuckled—"sorry about the play on words—Granny will be safe. In the meantime, Thor, myself, and the Big Guy are watching out for her."

Thor was about to say something when Baskerville bounded up the stairs. Around his mouth was what looked like a white beard. Trailing after him were Fish, Little White Poodle, Furball and Tank as Granny called the last two. They too had white beards. Before anyone could stop them, Baskerville ran to Starshine and started licking her cheek deposting part of the white beard on her face. Fish pounced on the table and rubbed his chin against Penelope. Little White Poodle jumped on Thor's lap, the poodle's beard flying onto Thor's face. Furball and Tank split up, Furball landing on Granny's head. The white beard fell off of his chin onto Granny's face. Tank made a jump for Franklin's lap and landed smack dab against his chest, wiping his white beard on Franklin's black shirt.

In the midst of the chaos, Angel came upstairs and threw herself in her mother's lap and hid her head. "I pretended to be Granny and fed all of them the dinner that was in the fridge. Did I do a good job? Am I in trouble?"

With those words, everyone looked at each other and started laughing, wiping cheesecake off of their faces.

"I take it this is dessert?" Thor managed to say through his laughter as he took a swipe of the white now on his face and put it into his mouth. Heather, who was sitting next to Thor, reached over and took a swipe from his face and put it into her mouth looking at Thor with a twinkle in her eye.

Granny, seeing the look, thought her plan might be working although she didn't plan this. "Yes, this is my famous 'Peanut Butter Cup Cheesecake' served with a dash of bark and bite." Granny turned to Angel who was still sitting in her mother's lap hiding her head. "And, no, you are not in trouble, Angel. Those shysters and Baskerville like sweet things and that is why they like you." Granny pushed herself away from the table and stood up.

"Since dessert is over, it's time for everyone to go, except Franklin. I need to talk to him. Thor, could you take Heather and Angel home for Franklin?"

Franklin gave Granny a strange look. "I can take them home and come back," Franklin offered, a little confused.

"No, I really need to talk to you." Granny grabbed his arm. "It's just, just, I feel a little unsafe tonight what with all the talk. I'm sure having you here for a little while longer until the talk goes out of my mind and the fear goes away will make me feel better." Granny leaned a little against Franklin to get her point across.

Penelope and Starshine winked at each other. "Right, you want to be alone. Because you're scared," Penelope stated. "Well, we could stay," she offered in a teasing voice.

Granny stared her down. "No! I need Franklin who is big and strong." Granny looked up at him, wondering if she got the adoring look part down to convince him.

"We'll take Heather and Angel home." Starshine offered. "We go right by her house."

"That would be better, Mom," said Thor. "I have to check on Elena. Have a good night, Heather. Sweet dreams Angel." Thor grabbed his coat before Granny could say anything more. Granny stared at the door as it closed behind Thor.

Quickly, she let go of Franklin. "I feel a lot better now. Must have been the air coming into the house. It breathes the fear right out of me. You can all go now. Franklin you can take Heather home. I need my beauty sleep. Thank you for coming." Giving Angel a quick hug, she ushered the confused group out of the house.

Granny locked the doors, grabbed her knitting needle cane and umbrella and called it a night. Tomorrow was another day and she had to come up with a plan to make Fuchsia safe again.

CHAPTER TWENTY THREE

Granny's eyes opened and she quickly sat up in bed and grabbed her throat. She let out a sigh of relief when she realized that there was nothing wrapped around her neck and strangling her. She had been dreaming that weeds had crawled up her body and wrapped themselves around her neck. She remembered gasping for breath and hearing Sally say, "The weeds have quit talking to me."

Granny heaved another sigh of relief. She looked toward the window and saw that it was daylight. Grabbing her cell phone, she checked the time. It was 8:00 a.m. Last night must have worn her out.

She looked down at her wintertime attire. Perhaps, that is why she felt she was being strangled. The warm, though colorful clothes fit snuggly around her neck to keep her warm. It was time to go back to wearing her *Sexy Granny and I Know* it pj's or some of her more colorful but scanty and freeing nighties. She would buy an electric blanket or wear her cuddly shyster robe to bed to keep warm.

The pillow and bed still felt warm and welcoming. Granny propped up her pillows to lounge a little longer. As she did, she thought back to her dream and realized the weeds strangling her was so real. *What did it mean? Why plant weeds in Sally's back yard?* Granny sat straight up in bed. *Could it be?*

Granny swung her feet to the side of bed and into her goose-feathered slippers. She bounded down the hall to her trash can and started dumping the trash. When the weeds that she had taken out of Sally's coat pocket dropped out to the floor, Granny picked them up and looked at them carefully. She turned back to her bedroom, walked down the hall deep in thought and sat down on her bed. After a few minutes, she went to her closet and threw on the first clothes she could find.

Once back in the living room, Granny pulled out her binoculars and aimed them at Sally's house. The hussy was home. Granny then trained the binoculars on Mavis' house. Mavis and George were up. Granny went back to her bedroom and grabbed her cell phone.

"Mavis, I need your help."

"Why, yes, Granny; we are fine. It is so nice of you to check."

"George is in the room with you?" Granny asked.

Mavis whispered, "Yes."

"I need you to go over and distract the floozy next door. I have to look at her weeds."

"Why I would be happy to check on Elena. It is nice of you to be concerned since her shade is crooked."

"Thanks; once I see you have her occupied inside, I will sneak over. Give George some food so he won't see me. When he's eating, he seems to forget anything else." Granny cut off the connection.

She picked up her binoculars and watched as Mavis entered Sally's yard and knocked on the door. The hussy/floozy answered and invited her in. Granny watched a few minutes more until they were out of sight of the window. Granny grabbed the green coat, reminding herself that she had to go shopping to find her own coat. Granny checked to make sure no one was watching as she hurried across the street to Sally's back yard with the weeds in her hand.

Once Granny was in the back yard, she took the weeds and put them next to the brown weeds that were shriveled up because of the weather. They weren't the same kind of weeds. Where did Sally get these weeds and why were they in the pocket of Sally's coat? It had to have something to do with the murders. She needed to talk to the Big Guy.

Granny toddled over to the front door and knocked. The hussy answered. "What do you want?"

"George told me Mavis was here and I was hoping she could give me a ride to town. I need to purchase a fall and winter coat." Granny angled her head around the body of Elena and looked straight at Mavis. "Now, if it's possible."

"Yes, yes; thank you, Elena. You were so helpful. The next time George sulks, I will use your advice." Mavis walked to the door.

Elena was about to let her pass to the outside when a voice behind Granny asked, "And what are you doing here so early in the morning, Mom and Mavis?"

Granny jumped at the sound of Thor's voice. Mavis hurried past all of them out the door. "I'll warm up the car," she said as she hurried down the steps.

"Don't worry, Thor," Elena said sweetly as she smiled at Thor. "It's all fine. Your mother was just apologizing to me for yesterday. Weren't you, Hermiony? After all, we all need to learn to get along now that I am in your life, Thor. She has realized that. Haven't you, Hermiony?"

Granny was wishing she had her cane with her. She would have made a point with the hussy that the hussy wouldn't forget. Granny looked at Thor. "Got to get to town. Want a lift?"

"No, I'm good. I bet Elena can find me some coffee." Thor kissed his mother on the cheek and walked through the door. Elena made a little wave to Granny and shut the door, leaving Granny standing on the steps.

A beep sounded from the street. Mavis was waiting. "I need to get my cane," Granny yelled at Mavis as she sprinted back to her house to grab her pink knitting needle cane.

"You never know when a good cane will come in handy," Granny explained to Mavis as she got in the car.

Mavis drove her usual 10 mph into town. Granny closed her eyes and took a little snooze along the way. She knew there was no hurrying Mavis.

"Where do you want to be dropped off?" Mavis asked, disturbing Granny's little nap. "I need to see the Big Guy so drop me off at the police station."

"Do you want me to wait for you at Ella's?"

"No, I have some undercover work for you to do."

"Me? Me?" Mavis squeaked in excitement.

"Yes, you. I need you to spy on Thor. I want to know how much he is seeing that floozy. I need to put a stop to it." Granny stepped out of the car and turned back to Mavis, "Oh, and don't tell George or Franklin or Thor or my daughters. Got it?" Granny slammed the door and walked into the police station in search of the Big Guy.

The Big Guy happened to be standing in front of the police station talking to Franklin. They both saw Granny at the same time.

"Franklin, what are you doing here?"

Franklin winked at Granny. "Just conferring about the case. Feels good to be consulted about this. I didn't realize how much I missed my detective days in New York. Cornelius was telling me a little bit about his life before he came here," Franklin explained. "What are you doing here?"

"I need to talk to the Big Guy too. Alone." Granny winked at Franklin.

The Big Guy shook his head. "Will you two quit winking in front of me? The last girl I winked at I arrested for stealing my wallet."

"How about dinner tonight, Hermiony? I'll pick you up at 6:00 since you no longer have a car. We can plan our wedding." Franklin chuckled at the expression on Granny's face. She certainly made his heart beat faster. She was so feisty. He did miss his mother and her zany outlook on life. She would approve of Granny because she was so much like her, but how was he going to get Granny to take him seriously?

"Fine, fine," Granny agreed, anxious for Franklin to be on his way so she could talk to the Big Guy.

"Franklin, that, ah, matter we talked about regarding the Nail case. See what you come up with when you visit the courthouse. I appreciate the help," the Big Guy called out to Franklin as Franklin was walking out the door.

"Now, Granny, let's go back to my office and we can talk."

Once seated in the Big Guy's office, Granny pulled the dead weeds out of her pocket and plunked them on the desk.

"Um, what do we have here?" the Big Guy asked Granny with a puzzled look on his face. "It looks like dead weeds."

"Not just any weeds, but weeds from the pocket of this coat that formerly belonged to Sally. I threw it on to cover my nightclothes when I was checking on Sally the day she died."

The Big Guy patted Granny's hands that were on the desk. "Granny, Sally was always pulling and cutting weeds. There is nothing suspicious about that."

"But there is," Granny said emphatically while pulling her hands from the Big Guy's grasp. "These are not the same weeds that covered her yard. Do you know what they are?"

The Big Guy studied the weeds a little more carefully. "Ah, no. Do you?"

"NO!" Granny yelled. "That's why you're the detective."

The Big Guy walked around the desk and helped Granny to her feet. "I think you should go over to Ella's, see Delight, have some coffee and then go home and rest. I think the past few months have been tough on you. You're seeing things in weeds; pretty soon you are going to tell me that the weeds are talking to you."

Granny stood up straight and stuck out her chin at the words, "the weeds are talking to you." "They are! They are! I heard them in the hussy's back yard when I was sitting on the ground in the middle of the weeds looking at the stars one night. They are! That's it! There has to be some connection."

The Big Guy's eyes narrowed into a squint as he looked at Granny.

"You need to investigate, Big Guy," Granny urged.

"Time for coffee, Granny. I'll escort you there myself." The Big Guy took Granny's arm, walked her through the station and next door to the fire hall. He found a table for Granny. For some reason that he couldn't explain, she wasn't protesting. He called Delight over.

"Hi, Granny; Hi Cornelius," Delight greeted them in an excited mood. "Did you see my teapot and coffeepot building has started? I think it will be ready by Christmas, sooner than we thought."

"Why don't you tell Granny all about it? I have to get back to work. I have a crime to wrap up." The Big Guy looked at Delight. "Keep an eye on her. I am going to call Mavis to come and pick her up. She needs some rest."

Delight and Granny watched the Big Guy leave. Granny turned to Delight. "I have to go. I don't want coffee. It's great about your shop. But I have a crime to solve." At that moment Granny's cell phone rang. It wasn't *Dragnet* but a strange number. Granny answered cautiously.

"Hello?"

"Granny, it's me, Mr. Pickle. I know you're not supposed to be working right now, but food is disappearing left and right and I can't figure it out and it happens right around this time. I haven't seen anyone suspicious. Mostly old ladies—sorry, Granny—I mean older women and they always leave through the checkout and buy something. I won't tell anybody if you don't tell anybody that I've put you back on the job."

"Granny turned away from Delight and whispered in her phone, "I'll be right there." Then in a loud voice she said, "What, Mavis, your car is in front of AbStract?. I should meet you there?" Granny hung up the phone and said to Delight, "I have to meet Mavis by AbStract."

Granny picked up her cane and walked out the door going in the direction of AbStract in case anyone was looking. As soon as she was by the alley, she made a swift right and walked around the building and headed the other way to Pickle's Grocery.

Mr. Pickle was waiting by the door as Granny entered. He gave a nod as Granny grabbed a shopping cart to walk around the store. She put her cane over the top of the cart in case she needed it. She started meandering down the aisles, picking an item here and there to throw into her cart so she would look like a shopper. Mr. Pickle was right. The entire store at this moment consisted of women like her trying to decide what delicious morsels they would like to purchase.

Granny's cart was almost full. The problem with doing this was that she found too many things to purchase and unless Mr. Pickle would deliver to her house she would have to forgo this many treats. She really did have to look into getting a new car as soon as the arson investigation was over and she got her insurance money.

Granny turned the corner and looked to the back of the store where the large orange juices in plastic bottles were arranged. Granny didn't need any orange juice but the yogurt was arranged on the shelf right underneath the bottles of orange juice. The shysters were almost out of yogurt so Granny decided she would purchase some. As Granny started down the aisle, an old woman with red hair and slim build came into view. She seemed to have hidden pockets in her coat and was shoveling the yogurt into those hidden pockets.

Could it be? It couldn't, Granny thought. *The woman looked like Gram Gramstead.* But that woman was in prison—or had she broken out? The nightmare woman was back and she was stealing yogurt.

Granny stopped her cart, picked up her pink knitting needle cane. She flipped the rubber end off of the bottom of the cane to reveal the sharp end. Granny moved next to her cart and stealthily shuffled a few footsteps down the store. With cane/knitting needle in her right hand, she lifted it and put it in javelin throwing mode. When she was ready, she let loose a yell and aimed the knitting needle at the woman who looked like her old nemesis Gram Gramstead.

The giant knitting needle flew through the air, hitting a large orange juice bottle and sticking in it, puncturing the side of the bottle. The bottle flew off the shelf, knitting needle and all. Orange juice poured out of the bottle onto the head of the unsuspecting suspect throwing her off balance and landing her on the floor.

Granny reached for her Big Guy alarm that was usually at her waist, before remembering the Big Guy had taken it away from her. As Granny moved toward the suspect, she started hollering, "Fire! Fire! Fire!" She heard the alarm go off.

The look alike Gram Gramstead was on the floor trying to get up but she kept slipping in the orange juice. Granny still had her handbag which was always with her and plunked it down on top of the woman's head. As the handbag brushed the woman's head, her red hair slid to the ground, uncovering her head to reveal Tricky Travis Trawler.

"Tricky Travis? What are you doing pilfering from Mr. Pickle? Didn't I skewer you just a few weeks ago? You didn't learn your lesson then?"

By this time, Mr. Pickle had arrived and Granny could hear the fire engines pulling up outside. "Here's your culprit. Didn't have my alarm. The Big Guy should be right behind the fire guys." Granny grabbed her giant knitting needle cane and pointed it at Travis' chest. "One word that I am the one who caught you, and I will find you in church the next time, and skewer your hand when you put it in the collection plate. Do you understand?" Granny warned Travis.

Travis looked at the needle pointing at his chest and at the skewered orange juice, gulped, and nodded yes.

"I'm not supposed to be here. See you later." Granny hurried out the back door, and proceeded down the different alleys until she found herself behind Rack's Restaurant. Straightening her clothes and adjusting her hat, she pushed open the door to Rack's to have lunch. She thought perhaps some good fried chicken and onion rings along with dessert would give her some time to think about her next step.

CHAPTER TWENTY FOUR

Rack's wasn't too busy. Many of the folks who had been having their lunch rushed out to see where the Fuchsia Fire Department was going. It wasn't unusual for the folks in Fuchsia to follow the fire trucks, especially now that there had been two recent fires that possibly had been arson. If asked, the residents of Fuchsia would tell you that they weren't being nosy but were concerned about their fellow residents and the safety of the firefighters. Of course, if they could find out a little gossip along the way, that never hurt anyone either.

As Granny waited for her food, she looked across the street at Mrs. Periwinkle's former house. Granny missed seeing Esmeralda feeding the birds in her yard, the yard that now was filled with dead weeds. Granny pulled out her cell phone and looked at it thoughtfully.

A spark of interest lit up her eyes when she remembered that she could connect to the internet with her Itphone. That was something she hadn't tried yet. Perhaps she could recognize the type of weed that had been in Sally's coat. Granny typed 'unusual weed' into the search engine. She studied the weed pictures one by one, holding the phone close to her eyes since the screen was so small. She was so engrossed in the pictures on the phone that she didn't even notice the waitress talking to her or setting her food down in front of her.

All of sudden, Granny sat up straight. She found it. Granny was so excited that she dropped her Itphone and it landed right smack in the middle of the gravy that was splashed over her mashed potatoes. Granny picked up the phone and wiped it off with her napkin. It appeared to be no worse for wear. Granny peered at the screen and then looked at Mrs. Periwinkle's yard.

Pulling some money out of her wallet, Granny took a few more bites of chicken and then threw the money down on the table and left by the front door, making sure none of her loyal watchdogs had caught up with her yet.

Crossing the street to Mrs. Periwinkle's, Granny had the time to note that the fire trucks were still apparently at Pickle's Grocery as the streets were still deserted. It always did take the residents of Fuchsia a little time to disperse after an exciting event. Granny was glad she could provide them with a little excitement once in a while.

As Granny walked to the back of the house, she heard a ruckus. There was growling and hissing going on. Granny got her cane ready in case she needed to defend herself. Rounding the corner to the back yard, the perpetrators of the noise became apparent to her. It was the shysters, minus Baskerville. Granny surmised that there might be more surprises waiting for her when she got home in the form of Mr. Bleaty courtesy of Baskerville.

The shysters were digging and pawing at the ground further along by the house. It didn't appear they were making much of a dent in the soil as no dirt was being scattered, just weeds—possibly, Granny surmised by a glance—because the ground might be partially frozen.

"Fish, Little White Poodle, Furball, Tank, you're going to end up in the animal hoosegow again if you don't quit this digging in other people's yards," Granny scolded as she approached them. They kept on digging.

Granny thumped the ground with her cane to let them know she meant business. When she did that, she hit something that made a noise and sounded solid. Leaning down, she took a better look. With the weeds all scratched off of the ground, she could see a solid, heavy, old wooden door, level with the ground. There were also remnants of grass that had been planted over the door so it covered it in its entirety.

"What have we here? Scratch some more," Granny instructed the shysters. The shysters continued their scratching, revealing the entire door.

As the door was revealed, Granny could see hinges. She bent down and tried to pry the door open with her fingers. It did not budge. The hinges were rusty and it appeared as if it hadn't been opened in many years.

" I think it's an old storm cellar, shysters, that's been there a long time. No mystery here. Go on home before we all get in trouble."

Fish planted himself by her leg and purred. Little White Poodle started yapping and headed toward the garage out back. Furball and Tank took that moment to lay down by the basement window and take a rest. Granny looked at the basement window to see if it was still open so she could get back in the house. Someone had nailed it shut.

Granny sat down on the cold ground to rest a spell and studied the house and yard. She had never noticed it before, but the house and yard were an exact replica of Sally's place. Granny wondered if they had been built around the same time by the same builder. She leaned closer to the ground to study the dead weeds. They were not the same as the ones in Sally's pocket. But the weeds were talking to her. Granny could hear voices that were muffled but sounded like they were shouting. Granny sat back up and looked around. There was no one around and when she sat up, she couldn't hear the voices.

It was at that time that Granny noticed the same type of cistern and pump that Sally had. Using her cane to hoist herself off of the ground, Granny stood up and walked to the cistern. Leaning down, she tried to move the lid but it was tight and no match for her weight.

Little Poodle and Tank started barking. Granny looked up to see the Big Guy walking around the side of the house toward her.

"What are doing here Granny? I thought Mavis was giving you a ride home."

"I was on my way to AbStract when I heard a noise as I was coming out of Rack's after lunch. It sounded like the shysters were around and I thought I better check. Low and behold, I found them here." Granny explained with her most innocent face. "Can you give us a ride home? I think they've been in enough trouble for the day and Baskerville is missing. And what are you doing here?"

"Just checking to make sure Neil isn't around here yet. We're keeping an eye on this place although we don't think he'll come back here. I fear he's gone for good." The Big Guy turned and looked at the house. "I thought maybe I'd make an offer on it. It's close to town and I can keep an eye on business this way." He walked over to Granny and took her arm that was holding her cane to escort her to the front of the house and his squad car.

Granny tried to pull away and walk by herself but he had her arm in a death grip and was hustling her to the squad car so fast her feet almost didn't touch the ground. The Big Guy didn't say a word all the way to Granny's house. At least, Granny thought he wasn't in so much of a hurry to get rid of her that he put the flashing lights and siren on to get her home, although that might have been exciting.

After the Big Guy dropped Granny off with the orders to stay put in her house until Franklin picked her up for their dinner date, Granny decided it was too early to get ready and she might have a little time to sort this mystery out.

Reaching into her refrigerator, Granny pulled out food for the shysters since their dishes were empty. As she did that, she noticed that she had left one little leaf from Sally's pocket on the floor of the kitchen by the trash can. Since the Big Guy probably had tossed the leaves that she had given him away she picked up the last leaf for safe keeping in case she needed it for evidence. Granny wondered how the Big Guy hadn't known what the leaf was. She realized in all the excitement with the shysters in Esmeralda's yard that she had forgotten to tell him what the weed was.

Granny picked up her cell phone to call him when a distant thought seemed to be running through her head. She couldn't seem to catch it though. She put down the cell phone and looked out the window to see if Baskerville was anywhere to be seen. Mr. Bleaty didn't seem to be in sight either.

Walking away from the window, Granny spied a collar lying on the floor. She picked it up and examined it. It hadn't been there in the morning. She recognized it as Mr. Bleaty's collar. It had chew marks on it. It looked like Baskerville had chewed the collar off of Mr. Bleaty. Fingering the collar, Granny sat down in her chair and thought back to her previous visits to Sally's back yard. It was strange that she hadn't noticed that the Periwinkle house and Sally's house were the same. Granny got up out of her chair with a look of determination in her eye.

Picking up her phone, she first dialed Mavis. "Mavis, do you know where Thor is?"

"Yes, he left a little while ago with Elena. Why do you want to know?" Sally asked suspiciously.

"Mr. Bleaty left something here and I need to return it. I didn't want any trouble from that hussy so I will deposit it by her garage in the back."

"Do you want me to come with you?"

'No, Mavis, I have a hunch so I'm calling the Big Guy and then I'll return the collar. See you later." Granny hung up the phone before Mavis could answer her.

Granny texted the Big Guy and told him the name of the plant; it was easier than calling him and having to submit to his nosiness. He might ask what she was going to do and where she was going. She'd be back before Franklin picked her up. No one would be the wiser.

Making sure her cell phone was in her pocket, Granny picked up her cane and her pocketbook, but then put her pocketbook back down. Carrying too many things might slow her down. She had to be quick so the hussy didn't see her. Granny grabbed the collar and hooked it over her arm. That would provide a good excuse in case she was found on the property. Stepping outside onto her porch, she looked around the neighborhood to make sure the coast was clear. *Once this mess was all cleaned up,* she thought, *she would make sure that Thor found a nice sweet, quiet girl to date.*

Once on the hussy's property, Granny decided she should check out the basement window to see if there was any progress in the basement. Granny peered into the window. There was just enough light in the basement to see that a door had been positioned in the wall where the cut in the wall had been.

Granny stood back up and walked to the back of the house. It seemed strange to have a door in the wall that went to nowhere except ground unless the hussy was planning to add on to her house at a later date.

Once in back, Granny examined the ground and the weeds next to the house. There was a patch that looked like it had been scraped or dug away. The shysters must have been here too. Granny knelt down to scrape more away. Sure enough, there was another wooden door. She tried to scratch more of the dirt and weeds away but she didn't have the right tools such as the shysters' paws and claws.

Granny sat down on the ground to think about this strange turn of events. These houses were older and many houses in the early days of Fuchsia had a tornado cellar, even though Granny had not lived here when the cellars were used. She had still been on the farm and they too had had a tornado cellar. But if these houses had basements, why did they need a tornado cellar? It was time for a trip to the courthouse to see if she could find anything in the archives about these two houses.

A car drove into the driveway and stopped. She could hear voices as someone got out of the car. It was Thor and the hussy. Granny turned and ran across the side lawn away from the driveway and into the forest. She would wind her way back to her house. This time she did not take time to stop and enjoy the forest. She could tell her toes were starting to turn blue. Fall certainly was winding down into winter.

Once Granny made it through the forest and over to her side of the street, she took a peek to make sure Thor and the hussy were not watching. Thor's car was gone and Granny watched as the hussy drove her car out of the driveway and down the street. She then hurried into her house to get ready for her dinner date with Franklin.

As Granny was debating whether to wear red or fuchsia for her meeting with Franklin, her cell phone started chiming *Dragnet*. Grabbing the phone, it took her a minute to answer the new-fangled device. She slid the lock free and bellowed into the phone, "I'm not ready yet."

"That's good, Hermiony," Franklin answered back, "I have to cancel, and something has come up with the case that I have to check out. Granny, I'll be out of town for a few hours."

Granny thought for a moment. "Franklin, remember the plans of Fuchsia that you examined before I hooked those crooks? Were there any tunnels across the street from me?

"No, those houses across the street had tornado shelters that were abandoned and the doors sealed and grass planted on top. They weren't connected to the underground streets. The houses had been raised up and basements built underneath them so the tornado shelters were no longer needed." Franklin paused. "Ah, Hermiony, why are you asking?"

"No reason; you know me—an inquiring mind, so I inquired."

Franklin belted back through the phone, "We almost have this case taken care of. Stay put. Lock the doors. Don't go anywhere until I get back. Do you understand?"

"Why I am so disappointed by our dinner cancellation that I will just lie in bed and eat bon bons." Granny lifted her eyes to the heavens and shook her head. "By the way, have you seen Baskerville today? I saw the shysters earlier but they haven't arrived here yet."

"Got to go, Hermiony. I'm sure they are fine. Stay out of trouble!" The line went dead.

Granny was about to put her cell phone down when it came alive with another ring. Granny picked it up and answered it to see Thor's face on her phone. She never would get used to people being able to see her when they talked to her on the phone. He looked a little stressed.

"Trouble with your love life, Thor?" Granny asked with a smile and a smirky tone.

"My love life is fine, that's why I'm calling. Elena and I will be out of town for the evening. The only reason I am telling you this is because you need to stay home and stay put. Remember, we don't know where Neil Nail is and your life may still be in danger. Talked to Franklin and he said he has to go out of town on a case. Checked with the Big Guy and he just got a report of a missing child and his entire department might get called out on it. For once in your life, listen to us. We do have Mavis watching your house but she seems a little flaky tonight, something about light shining from a hole in the ground and she is sure it was an alien attack." Before Thor gave her a chance to respond he hung up.

Everyone seemed to be leaving town. Granny walked over to her footstool to unearth her bottle of wine and pour herself a glass. It was too early to go to bed. The shysters and Baskerville hadn't made it back to keep her company. There seemed to be plenty of excitement elsewhere but not here. Granny wondered if there was something she could do to find the missing child. The child had probably wandered over to the Starcade. That was usually where they found missing kids. The Starcade had bouncy houses and old-fashioned pinball games. Kids seemed to be fascinated by the old machines banging and clanging.

Lifting her binoculars and peering out the window, Granny could see that the hussy was not home.

Darkness had fallen and the hussy's house was totally dark. In fact, Granny's house seemed to be the only house in the neighborhood with lights on. Even Mavis and George had their lights out. Perhaps they had traveled downtown for dinner.

As Granny trained the binoculars into Sally's backyard, there appeared to be little slivers of light shining into the sky from the backyard. Granny could not tell what it was. She hadn't seen it before. Maybe she should check it out, after all everyone was gone or busy and she could snoop unencumbered.

The words, "Stay put" echoed in Granny's mind. Of course, she reasoned, Franklin meant, stay in the neighborhood. Of course, that's what he meant. He didn't say, "Don't go over to Sally's house." He didn't say, "Don't go look for Baskerville." Maybe Baskerville was with Mr. Bleaty in the garage. Franklin did say, "Don't go anywhere." She wasn't going anywhere, she was going somewhere—to Sally's house.

Yup, Granny made up her mind. She could go to Sally's house. Then she remembered, both Franklin and Thor had done all the talking. She hadn't agreed to anything. With a smile and a little lilt to her step, Granny grabbed her cell phone. since she thought she might need the nifty flashlight feature, and picked up her pink knitting needle cane. Opening the door, she remembered it was cold outside, so she grabbed Sally's green coat that she had thrown on a chair when she gotten back home. As Granny closed the door behind her, she took a breath of the cool crisp air. Minnesota was a great place to be with the changing seasons; besides, it was easier tracking a crook when it was winter because they left footprints. However, the fall was also a good time to lose those who were tailing you because the leaves blew in your path covering your steps. Yup, Granny was happy on this night to be a Minnesotan.

CHAPTER TWENTY-FIVE

As Granny walked down the driveway by Sally's house to get to the back yard and the strange light that seemed to be shining out of the ground, she glanced to her right. She thought she saw a little movement through the window of Mavis' house. Granny stopped for a second to peer at the window. It must have been a figment of her imagination because all seemed quiet now. It was too early for George and Mavis to be sleeping so Granny figured they were out on the town.

As Granny turned on the flashlight on her cell phone, she pondered Mavis and George' relationship. She didn't know much about either of them before they had moved to Fuchsia. They always seemed reluctant to talk about their past. As nosy as Granny was, she had left it like that. She wasn't too eager to talk about her past on the farm either.

The rustling of the leaves and snarky strange sounds seemed to be coming from some creatures ahead of her. It was so dark that she couldn't make out the shape of whatever was making the noise. She took a chance and aimed her flashlight at the noise. Baskerville and Mr. Bleaty had been found. They seemed to be up to some mischief here in the yard. Granny walked closer.

It appeared that the cover on the cistern was raised about about two inches on one end and Mr. Bleaty and Baskerville were trying to get it open. That was where the sliver of light had been coming from in Sally's back yard.

"Quiet down, you two! Let me look, maybe I can help." Granny knelt down by the cistern and peered through the opening. Whew, it certainly had a strange smell. She didn't hear any sounds, but there was bright light down in the hole. Granny could see through the crack that there was a ladder attached to the side so that someone could get down into the cistern. She didn't remember ever seeing light in Sally's yard before at night.

Granny stood up and shone her flashlight around the edge of the cistern. There didn't seem to be any handle to hold on to so she could pry it open. Lifting her knitting needle cane, Granny tried to wedge it to lift the cover. It seemed to be stuck where it was at.

Granny walked over to the side of the garage and tried the door. It was locked. That left out tools. Granny looked toward her house and thought perhaps she should go home and get her own tools. Maybe Mavis and George had tools in their garage. While she was deciding what to do about tools, she checked out the dark neighborhood. It still appeared as if she were the only one around.

Baskerville started nudging the top of the cistern again. Mr. Bleaty started butting the side of the cistern. Granny thought the smell of whatever was emanating from the cistern was urging them on. She chased them both away with her cane and walked around the cistern to the closed side. Putting her cell phone in her pocket and setting her cane on the ground, she moved to the cistern. With both arms she grabbed the side of the cistern cover and tried to pull it towards her. At the same time, Baskerville started jumping excitedly and howling. As he howled and jumped, he landed on the pump handle of the pump that sat by the side of the cistern. All of sudden, the cistern cover popped open against Granny, tumbling her to the ground.

Quickly, Granny looked around to make sure no one had heard the mournful howl. Everything was still dark. Granny retrieved her cell phone that had been jolted out of her pocket and grabbed her cane to help her get up off of the ground. She wondered if she should call someone like the Big Guy or Franklin. Then she remembered Franklin was out of town and the Big Guy was looking for a lost child. She would take a peek and then she would decide who to call.

Granny leaned over the Cistern wall. Now that the cover was up, she could see that the wall had been widened at some point in time. There didn't seem to be any water at the bottom and she could determine that because there was so much light at the bottom of the cistern. Turning around, she tentatively put one foot in the cistern to test to see if the ladder was safe. It seemed to be sturdy so she grabbed the side of the ladder and hoisted her other leg down, holding her cane tight against the ladder so it wouldn't drop.

She slowly made her way down the ladder. Looking up, she could see Baskerville and Mr. Bleaty looking down at her. There was no noise coming from the hole except for the sound of some kind of fan or something running. *What on earth could be going on?*

Granny felt her feet touch hard floor. She let loose of the ladder but not before glancing up to see Baskerville and Mr. Bleaty. Somehow seeing those two silly faces gave her courage to continue. She made sure her cane was ready before turning around to see how much space she had.

When she turned around, her eyes opened wide in surprise. She had to lean back against the ladder for balance. The strong smell made her a little woozy. She was looking into a large room that must have covered the entire space of the yard above. It was carved out with stone walls and shafts of steel holding up the ceiling. At the end, toward the house was a wall with a door. The room was filled with plants, plants with the same leaves as the leaves Sally had in her coat. Shaking herself out of her surprise, Granny took a quick glance around to make sure there was no one else there. It appeared only she and the plants occupied the space for the moment.

Granny slowly made her way to the door closest to the house. She put her ear to the door but heard no sound. Quietly she opened the door. The room was dark. Granny pulled out her cell phone and shone its flashlight around the room. This was the old tornado cellar. On the far wall next to the house was something built out from the house. It looked like a tiny room such as a closet. Granny continued into the room and walked over to a strange little built-in thingy. The wall appeared to be solid but as she felt around the edges she could feel tiny hinges. The door must pop open from the inside.

The hussy must be involved in this. Granny knew it. It was time to call someone. Granny lifted her cell phone to call but nothing happened. She looked at the bars on the cell phone. No service. She would have to go back up the ladder and call.

As Granny walked over to the ladder, she marveled at the setup. *Where did they get the electricity for the lights,* Granny wondered. Maybe they stole Sally's electricity and she had noticed and it had gotten her killed. This was why Sally thought the grass was talking to he—it really was. Granny chuckled when she thought about what type of grass Sally was talking about and she didn't even know it. The more she thought about it, the more she laughed. There had been more weeds in Sally's yard than she had known.

Before Granny started climbing the ladder, she happened to glance to the other end of the room and she saw an open space to what seemed to be a tunnel. The noises from the motors appeared to be a sophisticated ventilation system and it was running through the tunnel.

Her hands were on the ladder to start her climb when she looked up. Mr. Bleaty and Baskerville were no longer there. A little chill went through her bones. She knew it was the chill of trepidation because it was hot, hot, hot. The heating system had to be turned way up. She shook off the chill and raised a foot to take the first step when the lid of the cistern slammed down. She was still looking at the closed lid when the lights flickered and died.

Her hands on the ladder tightened; she clutched the cane that was plastered with her right hand to the side of the ladder. Granny's head did not move. Her eyes darted from side to side as she realized her dilemma. The chill was back. Granny stayed in that posture for a few seconds before she remembered something her mother always said, "When you're dead, you're dead, think of something to put on your tombstone that you want to be read."

Granny thought about her mother's words of wisdom and her tombstone and decided she wasn't quite ready for her epitaph yet. Holding her cane tightly with her right hand, she took her foot off of the ladder. She took the cell phone she had stowed back in her pocket before stepping on the ladder and turned on the flash light and turned the beam of light on the curved opening that she had noticed at the other end of the room that appeared to open to a tunnel. She flicked the rubber off the end of the cane and prepared to meet whatever lay ahead for her in the tunnel. It must be another way out.

Since the room stretched the entire length of the back yard and the cistern entrance had been close to the garage it only seemed reasonable that Granny had checked the part of the room toward the house. Making her way the short distance to the door-like opening in the wall in the dark wasn't too difficult until she got close to the generators running the ventilation system. Even with her cell phone flash light and cane to guide her, it was hard to wind her way through the plants to get to the door in the dark.

She was almost to the door when she tripped on something on the floor near the door. She heard what sounded like a groan as she came tumbling down on top of something that felt human. Granny scrambled to get back up, a little frightened—although if asked, she would never admit it. Flashlight and cane still in hand, she shone the flashlight on the lump she had fallen over. The lump groaned again. It was hard to hear next to the generator which was next to the lump. Granny jumped back in surprise. It was Neil Nail trussed up like a chicken going to slaughter. There was duct tape over his mouth.

Cautiously, Granny leaned down and pulled the duct tape off of Neil's mouth.

"Neil, how did you get down here? They have been looking all over for you?"

"Neil licked his lips where the duct tape had been stuck. "Untie me, Granny, we have to get out of here before they come back. I'll explain later."

Granny gave him a soft poke with the pointed end of her cane. "Not so fast; I wasn't born yesterday, you know—maybe the day before, but not yesterday. I'm not letting you loose until you tell me why you tried to poison me and why you burned down my garage."

"Granny, there is no time. I didn't do any of those things. At least untie my feet. We have to go. They are going to be coming back."

"Who are they?" Granny asked with a jab. At that moment, they heard the lid on the cistern trying to be lifted. "Neil Nail, I know you're not in this alone. I'm going to untie your feet and I'll help you up. We'll go and get help. But one try at a getaway and this giant needle will knit you right to the ground. Got it?" Granny warned in a tough voice, not letting on that perhaps she wanted to use her red sparkly running shoes to run down the tunnel and leave him behind.

They heard another clunk from up above. Granny, not knowing who it might be, untied Neil's feet and using her cane for leverage helped him to his feet. Shining her flashlight into the tunnel, Granny positioned Neil ahead of her by sliding the needle between his elbow and the side of his body of his tied arms.

Slowly and quietly, they started making their way through the tunnel. Granny whispered to Neil, "Do you know where this goes?"

"Yes," Neil whispered back, "It comes out on some private property on Bluebird Lake."

"Why does no one know about this?" Granny asked.

"Because there are 'No Trespassing" signs on this side of the lake and it is well hidden with trees and wild grass and growth. No one comes on the property because of the signs. And in Fuchsia, no one thinks that is strange and so they forgot about this property on this side of the lake. There is a little back road that leads to another back road. There are gates hidden in the woods so no one can use the road and it is well disguised from the other back road. That is how they get the merchandise out of here."

"This tunnel has to be long. It is at least a mile or two across the field from Sally's house to the lake."

Neil and Granny kept on walking in silence, listening for any sound behind them. They could see some light starting to appear in front of them. They were reaching the end of the tunnel.

"As soon as I can get some cell coverage, I'll call the Big Guy," Granny informed Neil as they were almost to the light. Neal was about to say something when they saw a large figure standing at the end of the tunnel.

When Granny saw who it was she exclaimed, "How did you find us? I was just going to call you for help. You should have never took my alarm from me!"

Neil, when he saw who it was, started to dive for the floor almost taking Granny with him. While Neil was diving for the ground, the knitting needle took a downward slant and slid from between his arm and side, leaving Granny holding the giant knitting needle.

"You found him!" the Big Guy exclaimed. "I got a tip that he might be hidden in this tunnel from the property owner, who said there had been people trespassing on his property. When you gave me the dried plant from Sally's pocket, I thought there might be a connection. I was right. Franklin did some research for me and found out about the tornado shelters in both houses. Neil, here has been using them for his pot growing operation."

The Big Guy moved forward.

"Granny, run! Don't believe him! He killed my father! He killed Sally, he killed Esmeralda, and he's going to kill you and me!" Neal yelled while trying to get up, but not being able to quite make it with his hands tied.

At that moment, another figure appeared at the end of the tunnel. "I see you found her, Father," said Elena to the Big Guy. She walked over to Neil and helped him up. "Honey, have you come to your senses yet?" She brushed Neil's cheek with her lips. "We had a good deal going here. Don't you see, we had to get rid of your father?"

Granny's grip tightened on her knitting needle cane. "You, Big Guy?" Granny asked in confusion and disappointment.

"Sorry Granny," replied the Big Guy. "I do like you but you are too nosy and too good at what you do, although most people wouldn't guess that. I had a great operation going in this town until Sally found that weed and came to me with her suspicions. She finally guessed, after all these years, that the grass really was talking to her." The Big Guy laughed. "From underground, that is, when we were taking care of our business."

"But Esmeralda?" Granny asked as she put the cell phone back in her pocket unnoticed and pressed the record button since there still was no cell signal. At least, after she was gone, maybe they would find her cell phone and know the truth. She had to buy some time to think of a way to get out of this, and she wanted to know the entire story before the epitaph was written on her tombstone.

"Those two women would still be alive if they would have accepted my offer to buy Sally's house and Neil's offer to buy that Mrs. Periwinkle's." The hussy Elena chimed in.

Granny glared at the woman standing next to the Big Guy. "You're his daughter?"

"I am. It's a family business. When he moved to Fuchsia to take this job, he bought the land by the lake to expand our business operation," Elena explained.

"I didn't know about the tunnels to the two properties until after I bought the property," explained the Big Guy. "I was going to build some camouflaged buildings to hide the growing operation and then when I was scouting the property, I found one of the tunnels."

"Dad called me and I did some research on Sally's property and talked to a son of the first property owner.

This man was well into his 90's but he told quite a story that had never been documented. It appears that in the middle 1800's, these two properties—Sally's and Esmeralda Periwinkle's—were used in the Underground Railroad to hide slaves on their way to freedom in Canada." The hussy looked at her dad when she finished speaking.

He continued: "I found the other tunnel and followed both tunnels and found the huge rooms under the property. I had to tweak them a little and also cut a door utilizing the tornado shelters too. Sally and Esmeralda had no clue. Esmeralda didn't spend much time in her yard and no one believed Sally about the grass talking because she was so ditzy."

Granny knew she had to keep them talking. Neil was also quiet, listening to what was being said. "You have electricity. It's quite a setup."

"Took me a while to figure that out but it is quite the operation. But it's time to quit talking." The Big Guy lifted his arm to reveal a gun.

At that moment, there was another burst of energy from behind the Big Guy. He stood his ground but the hussy turned around to see what was happening. She too had pulled a gun.

The shysters ran into the tunnel, barking and meowing and following them was Angel.

Granny's heart almost jumped out of her chest. She moved quickly and grabbed Angel. "Sweetie, what are you doing here?" she asked while keeping an eye on the Big Guy, his daughter and their guns.

"I followed my pets. We were playing and then I got losted following them and I got scared. But I kept following them cause I didn't want them to get losted." Angel looked up at the Big Guy. "It's not nice to point play guns at people. My mommy told me that."

Granny bent down to talk to Angel. "Honey I think it's time you go and take the shysters with you."

"I don't think so," the Big Guy remarked.

Granny looked up at the Big Guy with a withering look. She tightened her hold on her cane. As she used her cane to stand up, she took Angel's hand. Keeping her eye on the Big Guy and his daughter, Granny led Angel over to the side of the tunnel. In a loud voice, she said to Angel. "Sit down, honey." Granny called to the Shysters, "Fish, Little White Poodle, Furball, Tank, come here and sit by Angel."

The shysters actually listened. When they got over by Angel, Granny picked them up one by one and positioned them so they were covering Angel. Granny leaned down to kiss Angel on the cheek. As she did this, she whispered in Angel's ear, "Don't be scared but when you hear me yell 'run,' you and the shysters run out the entrance where you came in. Don't quit running until you find Franklin. Do you understand?" She stood back up and walked back to confront the Big Guy, standing next to Neil Nail.

"How are you going to get out of this, Cornelius? Killing an old woman, and a child?"

"First, lay the knitting needle down nice and slow, Granny. I don't need a hole in my heart." He and Elena both trained their guns on Granny.

"I am an old lady, Big Guy. I couldn't poke a flea with this. I pick up papers with the end. You know that; you've seen me," Granny said in a helpless voice trying to buy time.

"Down, Granny, or you will be seeing stars before you get the story and I am sure you want to know everything before you enjoy your rest in the Fuchsia Cemetery."

Granny, looking back at Angel and winking at Neil, gently put the cane down by her feet.

"I didn't kill you Granny, Neil did. Then he had such remorse for killing Sally, Esmeralda and his father and murdering you and setting the fires that he couldn't live with himself anymore and so he had to have some lavender tea to end it all," The Big Guy continued on. "It's such a great plan, Granny, and I have to thank you for solving my dilemma on how this was all going to end."

"Me?" Granny questioned. She turned and looked Neil straight in the eye and winked at him so the Big Guy couldn't see.

"I'm looking for a missing child. She is going to stay missing. Elena is going to leave and raise Angel now that those animals of yours got her involved in this. I don't kill kids. In fact, I have always wanted a granddaughter. She'll adjust."

"How does this explain the rest of the mess you're leaving behind?"

"I was looking for Angel and I stumbled upon these tunnels and Neil's pot growing operation. I found him and you. So sad. I got here too late. The fact that I found this on my land was just too much for me. I am going to have to move away from Fuchsia. The shock was just too much for me. I'll figure out a way for all to believe that Angel is dead too. A terrible accident in the marsh and her body can't be recovered. That's it, Granny. It's time. Gently lay it down on the ground. Do you have your epitaph written? You're going to need it."

The hussy who had been listening to all of this, moved forward right as the Big Guy raised his gun. "Wait, I ain't raisin' no kid. We need to rethink this." In her exasperation and her anxiety about what she had just heard, Elena stomped up to her father and stood in front of him. At that moment, there was a noise from the tunnel behind them.

"No, no! You can't shoot, you can't shoot! I won't let you!" At that moment, Mavis came running out of the tunnel brandishing a large stick. Neil took the surprise interruption and threw himself down, still with his hands tied, onto Elena, who toppled into her father knocking him to the ground. Granny swiftly bent down and grabbed her knitting needle cane as she yelled "Run, Angel, run!"

Angel and the shysters ran past the struggling group and out the entrance.

Granny took her knitting needle and stood on top of the Big Guy with her little body and pointed the knitting needle at his chest putting just enough pressure on the needle to go through his shirt and puncture his skin, holding it there so there was no doubt that Granny would skewer him to the ground if he moved.

"Mavis, I don't know why you're here but call Franklin and the police."

"She doesn't have to. We're here!"

Granny looked up to the see Franklin, Thor and the Fuchsia Police Department coming through the entrance to the cave.

"Angel's out there," Granny told Franklin still holding her needle to the Big Guy's chest.

"We have her, Hermiony. We'll take over, back off, slowly," said Franklin.

Thor reached down and grabbed the Big Guy and helped him up. He handcuffed the Big Guy's hands behind his back. "You're under arrest. You have the right to remain silent. Anything you say can and will be used against you in a court of law." Thor continued to recite the rights to the Big Guy as he led him out of the tunnel.

The policemen led the hussy and Neil Nail out behind Thor and the Big Guy.

Franklin walked over to Granny, looked her in the eye and then put his arms around her and pulled her into a big bear hug. "Woman, you are the most infuriating person I have met since my mother walked this earth. I don't know whether to shake you, lock you away or kiss you." With that he grabbed Granny and gave her a long kiss.

Shocked, Granny grabbed Franklin's arm for support when the kiss ended. She turned to Mavis who was standing, watching with her mouth wide open. "Mavis, how did you get involved in this?"

"I was supposed to watch you but I knew you would try and give me the slip, so I sent George out of town to his sons and I turned out my lights. I watched as you snuck into Sally's yard and as you found where the light was coming from. I tried calling Franklin and Thor but they wouldn't pick up so I left them a message."

"There was something moving in your house in the dark; I wasn't imagining it." Granny exclaimed.

"No, you almost saw me. When I saw that Baskerville and Mr. Bleaty accidently shut the cover on the Cistern and I couldn't reach Thor or Franklin by phone, I decided you might need help. I saw that the cistern cover was activated by the pump. I opened the cover door, grabbed a big stick and climbed down. I used my cell phone as a flash light. I could hear voices in the tunnel and as I got closer, I turned off my flashlight. I heard everything."

"Well you came out at the right time," Granny remarked. "It gave us the chance to get Angel out of here."

"I didn't even think. He was going to kill you. No one does that to my best friend."

Granny raised her eyebrows at the words *best friend*. She walked over to Mavis and took her hand. "Come on, Mavis, time to get you to your pretend reality show. It must be running late."

CHAPTER TWENTY-SIX

Once back at her house, Franklin settled Granny in her easy chair and got her a big bowl of ice cream and topped it off with a donut and a cup of hot cocoa which wasn't Granny's usual late night drink, but she didn't think she should complain. Her epitaph was going to wait awhile, although when her daughters got wind of this, perhaps it would have been easier having to change her residence to the Fuchsia cemetery rather than seeing what her daughters might have in store for her.

The shysters were back home too after leading Angel on a wild adventure that worried everyone in Fuchsia who had been looking for her. Angel was at home with her mother and tucked into bed for the night after relating her exciting adventure to her mother. Instead of fear, she was exuberant with excitement over having helped catch a crook.

Franklin refused to give Granny any more information about the case until Thor arrived after booking the Big Guy at the Big Guy's own police station.

"What did Thor have to do with all of this?" Granny asked. "And why did he arrest the Big Guy? He's not a cop."

"All in good time, Hermiony, all in good time."

A howl let out, the window door opened and Baskerville and Mr. Bleaty came into the house.

"Have you ever known anyone to have a goat for a pet in the house, Franklin?" Granny asked as Mr.

Bleaty came over and nuzzled her hand. Franklin's look gave Granny her answer. "He doesn't have a home now." Baskerville moved next to Mr. Bleaty and nuzzled him. "Baskerville and Mr. Bleaty seem to have a connection."

The door opened and Thor walked in. He walked over and gave his mother a kiss on the cheek. "What were you thinking?" he said to his mother in an exasperated voice. "What part of stay home, don't go anywhere, didn't you understand?"

Franklin started laughing. "We both should know those words are a challenge in Granny's ears; we should have told her to go out and investigate. Then maybe she would have stayed home."

"Thor, I don't understand. What authority do you have that you could arrest the Big Guy?"

"I didn't move here to keep an eye on you; however, you were the perfect excuse for me to move to town without any suspicion. I've always told you that I was a sales rep for a company and that is why I traveled. I work undercover for police departments and other organizations. They call me in to help them on cases. I moved to Fuchsia because I had been following Elena. There was always the suspicion that Cornelius Ephraim Stricknine was involved in some shady dealings at his last position as a police chief but it never could be proven. It was felt that somehow his daughter was also involved."

It took a lot to shock Granny silent, but this news certainly did. All Granny could do was stare at Thor with an open mouth.

"That's why you got involved with that hussy?"

Thor gave his mother a huge grin. "Yup and it was so much fun watching you try and stop me."

"But I don't understand; why did Mr. Nail die and why the weeds in the yards?"

Franklin took over the explanation. "Mr. Nail found out that Neil was involved and he confronted Neil. Mr. Nail had the lavender tea and the fertilizer tested after he found out about Sally and Esmeralda being poisoned with lavender tea and after he saw their yards. Neil had ordered the fertilizer and it had been Neil's idea to give them the lavender tea as a bonus. Mr. Nail confronted Neil and Neil told him it was part of the plan because Sally and Mrs. Periwinkle wouldn't sell their property. It was the Big Guy who sabotaged those shelves leading to Mr. Nail's death. That was enough to make Neil threaten to quit and blow the whistle on the Big Guy. So the Big Guy took care of Neil and hid him in the tunnel until Neil could be brought to his senses. It seems Elena really was sweet on Neil"

"The Big Guy and Elena and their group wanted the properties to make things easier for them. They planned on putting a door inside the house to the tunnel and using the basements for their business too. It would give them easier access to taking care of the plants," Thor explained.

"Neil was a long time resident of Fuchsia and Elena is a pretty, sweet young thing, so no one would suspect them. When the women wouldn't sell, the Big Guy was going to make sure their property looked decrepit so when the women were dead, Neil and Elena could get the property for a song using the condition of the property to drive down the value." Franklin looked at Granny as he continued. "They weren't planning on you suspecting anything."

Thor stood up and walked around the room as he explained more of the plan. "Elena didn't know who I was except that I was your son, and she was counting on me to keep you away from her since you keep such a good eye on your neighbors. It also didn't hurt for the community to accept her as my girlfriend."

Thor held out a piece of paper and gave it to Granny. "For whatever it's worth, Mom, the Big Guy wrote this and told me to give it to you."

Granny looked down at the letter and started to read out loud. "Granny, I didn't want it to end like this. But you are too good at being old and innocent and deceiving. You are too smart for things to get past you and even though I didn't want to hurt you, because you made my time in Fuchsia interesting, my scare tactics didn't work to keep you away from trying to solve crimes in Fuchsia. I am sorry about your cars and I am sorry about the poison when you were awarded the key to the city. I didn't give you enough to kill you but I thought possibly your nosy nose would be distracted and you would give up. I should have known that the Granny I have gotten to know over the years doesn't give up and when the community of Fuchsia has crimes that need solving, your amateur nose doesn't quit sniffing. I hadn't counted on how big your heart is and how much you care about the citizens of Fuchsia. Others may see you as a daffy, old lady but I know that you're not really that old and I know that you have many years of cunning deceit ahead of you. For what it's worth, stay safe. The Big Guy, Cornelius Ephraim Stricknine."

Granny looked at Thor and Franklin after reading the letter. Her eyes, although she would never admit it, had a little tear of sadness for someone who could have had a good future and who she had counted on over the years. The events of the evening also made her wonder about her skills of judging character. She hadn't guessed. Slowly, she put down the letter.

"I didn't know; I didn't guess. All these years and he had me fooled too."

Thor knelt down by Granny. "He was a model citizen, Mom. He did solve crimes. He was good to people, until it all fell apart. I think he thought he could move to Fuchsia, continue with his business and do some good too. The things he was suspected of being involved in were far worse than what you found today. He did turn his life around, just not all the way."

Granny looked down at her unfinished donut and lifted it to her mouth. With a glint in her eye, she turned to Thor and said, "You won't tell your sisters, will you? They don't know what you do either. I won't tell if you won't tell."

After Granny was able to convince Thor and Franklin to leave, she set out another bowl for Mr. Bleaty. Tomorrow she would have to take him to the vet and make sure he had whatever goats were supposed to have for shots and things. She decided she would build a goat barn on the other side of her house near the woods at the same time she rebuilt her garage. She wondered if goats liked bright pink. She had heard somewhere that goats liked tin cans. She would have to check on that. In the meantime, as she looked at Mr. Bleaty and Baskerville snuggled together sleeping on the rug, she decided he could stay in the house over the winter. He seemed to be housetrained, thanks to Baskerville.

With one last glance at the shysters as they were running out the door for their nightly excursions, she turned out the lights, donned her hot pink shorty nightgown and was about to crawl into bed when she decided that it was a miracle she was not in the wrinkle farm or ready to be put into the Fuchsia cemetery. Walking out into the living room, she dug in her footstool and grabbed her bottle of wine, along with a glass and took it to bed with her. She could be tipsy, topsy while she was lying in bed. Tomorrow was another day and who knew what would happen now that the Big Guy was no longer in Fuchsia. Maybe she should take his job. She would drink to that. She chuckled at the thought. Sitting in her cozy bed she held up her wine glass and gave a toast to events of the day.

CHAPTER TWENTY SEVEN

Granny opened one eye. She could see through the one eye. She squirmed a little and enjoyed the softness of the mattress before opening the other eye. The sun was up. Granny stuck her big toe out of the blankets to see what color it was. It wasn't red and it wasn't blue; it was in between. That must mean that it wasn't too cold out yet for her to need her new winter coat.

She listened to see if there were any sounds coming from her kitchen. Nope, it was safe to get out of bed in her purple leather pjs although it wouldn't matter if her kids had invaded her house. These days she always threw on her robe before venturing out into the other rooms since it was fall and there was always a chill in the morning.

It troubled her a little that she hadn't seen or heard much from her daughters since the Big Guy fiasco a couple of weeks ago. That in itself was a little suspicious. Maybe they were plotting and were waiting to descend on her with bad news. As those thoughts were racing through her head, the phone by the bed rang.

"Yup, I'm up," Granny said chuckling at her rhyme. She hadn't had to think about that one, it just happened.'

"Mom?"

Granny held the phone away from her ear and looked at it? Had she conjured up the phone call? Was she now telepathic?

"Yes, Penelope," Granny answered in a cautious tone.

"It's Sunday. Starshine and I thought we'd come over and attend church with you."

"You don't have to trouble yourself. I'm sure Butch would like you to go to church with him. I'll go with Mavis," Granny answered, alarmed at the offer of church with her daughters.

Her daughters didn't do church in Fuchsia, said they didn't like not knowing what type of service was going to be said. We Save You Christian Church was the only church in Fuchsia, so it took turns with worship services. Sometimes the services were Lutheran, sometimes Baptist, sometimes Methodist and on occasion, the Catholic Priest would come over and there would be a mass. It was never announced ahead of time. That is why the church pews were always full. People liked the idea of surprise at church.

"We insist. Since you don't have a car, we will pick you up in an hour. That should give us time to travel from our town to yours and still get a good seat in church." Penelope hung up the phone before Granny could protest.

Slowly, Granny left the warmth of her bed and shuffled to the bathroom to take a shower and do her hair. She dressed in the clothes that Mavis had given her on the day she was supposed to have gotten spa'd, opting to wear the wide-brimmed red hat that she had gotten from Mavis when she had spa'd Granny.

When Granny got to her kitchen, she made herself a cup of coffee with the Boneyard Coffee & Tea coffee beans that she had bought at Ella's Enchanted Forest and took out a lemon meringue donut she had saved from her last trip to Ella's. She would be glad when Delight had her new shop, all those firemen and policemen made it harder for Delight to fill Granny in on the happenings of Fuchsia.

In her reverie and savoring of her coffee and donut, Granny had forgotten about the time until she heard a horn toot outside her window. It was the girls. It looked warm enough to wear her new fall jacket. After skewering the Big Guy, she had finally had some time to herself so she could shop for her own fall and winter coat. She had appreciated borrowing Sally's coat but it still smelled like that weed, and green wasn't really her color. The purple fuchsia-lined fall coat with fuchsia buttons fit her personality much better. Granny grabbed her coat and cane and walked out to meet her daughters.

The parking lot at We Save You Christian Church was full. Granny looked for Travis Trawler. He didn't seem to be in church. She figured he must still be serving time in the hoosegow for pilfering yogurt from Pickle's Grocery. Starshine walked in to church and sat down halfway to the front. Penelope took her arm and led her to the pew.

As Granny was looking through the pages of hymns in the hymnal, Granny felt a tap on her shoulder. She turned around to see Thor and Franklin sitting behind them. A few rows up she saw Heather, Angel and Delight and Ella whispering in their pew. Granny looked across the aisle and met the gaze of Mavis. George was sitting next to her.

Pastor Hester Snicks started to speak so all whispering in the church ceased. The entire service seemed to fly by. The only hitch in the service was when Pastor Snicks started singing one hymn and the organ started playing another. Half of the congregation followed Pastor Snicks and the other half followed the organist. It was no wonder a dog started howling outside of church, a dog that sounded amazingly like Baskerville.

After the service, Granny was ready to jump up and blow the joint, but Pastor Snicks stopped her to talk. Everyone else seemed to hurry out of church away from their conversation. "Granny, how nice of you to join us again."

"Um, I'm here every week."

"Why yes, yes you are, I guess." He jumped in glee. "I rhymed just like you."

"You did. Got to go and catch my family." Granny started down the aisle.

Pastor Snicks grabbed her arm so fast she did a spin around on one leg."

Granny looked at him, raised her hands as if to say, "What?" and gave him a look of disbelief.

Pastor Snicks looked toward the doors at the back of the church. "You have to go now, Granny."

Again, Granny raised her hands in a questioning way. "Wasn't I trying to do that?" She stomped her cane on the floor of the church and turned and walked toward the outside double doors. She opened the doors and silence greeted her. The parking lot was entirely empty except for a 1957 red Chevy convertible that was sitting next to a 1957 black Chevy convertible. Since it was such a nice fall day, the tops were down. Standing next to the red Convertible was Franklin. The entire congregation, including her children, were gathered around the outside of the parking lot watching.

Granny was speechless until Thor came and took her arm and led her over to Franklin.

"What is this, Franklin?" Granny said in a crusty tone.

Franklin turned to Granny and opened a tiny box that he held in his hand. "Hermiony Vidalia Criony Fiddlestadt, you are the most maddening, stubborn, funny, exasperating person I have ever met even more than my mother. Will you marry me?"

Granny, looked at Franklin, speechless, a small tear uncharacteristic of Granny started in her eye. It took her a moment before she could find her voice. "Franklin, are you telling me that your black '57 Chevy convertible wants to share my garage with what I take it is my new red '57 Chevy convertible? Are you asking for Itsy and Bitsy to become Furball and Tank and team up forever with Fish and Little White Poodle? Are you asking for me to become Angel's grandma for real?"

Franklin answered seriously, "I am and I am willing to adopt Baskerville and Mr. Gottlieb. Does that mean yes?"

"Franklin, I need to tell you one thing before I say yes. I need to confess."

"Confess?"

"Yes, Mr. Gottlieb is a Mrs.," Granny said mischievously.

Franklin threw back his head and let out a loud laugh, grabbing Granny in a big bear hug, swinging her around in a circle, as the crowd started cheering and clapping.

Granny felt a tug at her dress when Franklin put her down. She and Franklin looked down to his granddaughter Angel tugging on her skirt.

Franklin leaned down and lifted Angel in his arms. "Did you have something you wanted to say, Angel?"

"Yes, Mommy and Thor said I can tell you our secret now. Granny is really going to be my Granny and Thor is going to be my Daddy."

Franklin and Granny looked over to where Heather and Thor had been standing. They were both grinning and holding hands. "What do you think, Mom?" Thor said with a teasing look in his eyes, "A double wedding at Christmas time?"

About the Author

 Julie Seedorf believes that if you believe it, you can do it. Julie retired from her computer business in 2014 to journey into writing full time. Putting her creativity to work, she is the author of the fictional Fuchsia, Minnesota Mystery series. Her first book *Granny Hooks A Crook* weaves a story about a fictional town in Minnesota that doesn't conform to the conventional rules and regulations of the communities that we live in today. Granny herself is unconventional and many say unbelievable. Perhaps she is only unbelievable because we have stereotypes of the way older people are supposed to age. Julie's books in the Fuchsia, Minnesota series are meant to poke fun at those ideas.

Adding to her career as an author, Julie also writes freelance human interest stories for Minnesota area newspapers, the *Albert Lea Tribune* and the *Courier Sentinel*. She hopes to expand her freelance career in the future. Seven years ago Julie started her career as a columnist. Her column *Something About Nothing* can be found in the *Albert Lea Tribune, the Courier Sentinel* and online at her blog http://www.sprinklednotes.com.

Having lived in small communities all her life Julie knows the richness that a small community can have in bringing up a family. Julie raised her children in small communities and takes the time to make sure her grandchildren learn the importance of the saying, it takes a village to raise a child.

The experiences of grandchildren learning who a grandparent was when they were young, is the subject of the *Granny's In Trouble* series that Julie writes with her grandchildren. The first book in the *Granny's in Trouble* series, "Whatchamacallit? Thingamajig?" was published in 2012. The next book in the series will be out soon.

You can find Julie on Facebook at http://www.facebook.com/sprinklednotes, on her blog sprinklednotes, on twitter at @julieseedorf or on her website at julieseedorf.com. Her books are available on Amazon, Createspace, Barnes and Noble and other independent bookstores.

31222255R00137

Made in the USA
Lexington, KY
03 April 2014